Parts
Unknown

Parts
Unknown

John Dilmore Jr.

CREATIVE ARTS BOOK COMPANY

Berkeley ∽ California 1999

For information contact:
Creative Arts Book Company
833 Bancroft Way
Berkeley, California 94710

Parts Unknown is published by Donald S. Ellis
and is distributed by Creative Arts Book Company

ISBN 088739-182-6
Library of Congress Catalog Number 98-71500

Printed in the United States of America

FOR MY PARENTS

ONE

LIVE BAIT

Carter Jackson was dreaming. His pupils darted back and forth beneath his eyelids like a pair of mice trapped under a rug. They ran left, then quickly to the right as in his dream Carter looked both ways before jogging across the street to the Bottleneck city garage, where his police cruiser was parked.

Jimbo Spell sat on a wooden bench in front of the cavernous building, reading that week's *Mingo County Times*. He folded the paper and stood up when he saw Carter.

"A few more miles and the engine would've locked up on you," he said, taking a set of keys from the pocket of his coveralls and tossing them to Carter. "You might wanna try adding a quart of oil next time you smell smoke."

Catching the keys, Carter walked over to the car. "I'll keep that in mind," he said, opening the door and getting in behind the wheel. He started the car and revved the engine, spinning the rear wheels as he pulled out onto the street.

Carter's mind raced ahead. He was several miles outside of town, making a left turn into the parking lot of Hotard's Grocery and Bait. The small gravel lot was empty except for a dusty black Camaro. Carter parked a car length behind the Camaro, which he noticed had an expired tag, and got out.

Taking a handkerchief from his pocket, he wiped the sweat from the back of his neck as he more closely examined the Camaro's license plate. He knelt at the rear of the car and rubbed gently at the upper portion of the plate's first digit with the tip of his finger. The paint that had been used to turn what was originally a U into a malformed O began floating away on the breeze. A number of the tiny paint chips blew into Carter's mouth. He spit them out as he got up and walked toward the store.

Inside, Billy Hotard stood behind the counter, wearing a sky blue bowling shirt with the name Kate stitched into the pocket.

"Afternoon," he said, tilting his head in Carter's direction.

"Hot one," Carter said, still swabbing the back of his neck. "You're keeping it nice and cool in here, though."

"I've got to. For the night crawlers."

Carter followed Billy's gaze to the back of the store, where a hand-painted sign reading LIVE BAIT hung on the wall. A tall, bearded man wearing torn jeans and a faded vinyl jacket stood beside a pyramid of small, cylindrical cardboard boxes with "$1.49" printed on their sides. The man held one of the boxes. He had removed the lid and was digging through the moist dirt inside with his thumb and index finger. Smiling, he pulled a long, fat worm from the dirt. He held it up to his face and looked past it, into Carter's eyes.

"Afternoon, Deputy," the bearded man said.

"Gonna do some fishing?"

"I'm thinking about it." The man stuffed the worm back into the box.

Carter's fourth-grade math teacher, Mrs. Delia Lodish, stepped from behind the soft-drink cooler. Carter looked down and saw that he was wearing only his gunbelt and a pair of white cotton briefs. His cheeks flushed as he turned to Billy, who had begun crying. Tears streamed down the merchant's thin face and dripped from his chin, spotting the front of his shirt.

Turning back to the cooler, Carter saw that Mrs. Lodish had been replaced by the bearded man. He was pointing a fat revolver at Carter's chest.

"Drop that iron, cowboy," he said.

Carter heard Billy sobbing behind him as he dropped his handkerchief and pulled his nine millimeter automatic from its holster. He fired at the bearded man as a shower of sparks erupted from the fat revolver's muzzle.

Waking, Carter lurched to a sitting position in his bed, his hand going to his side. He looked around his room for a moment, unsure of where he was until his eyes came to rest on the wrinkled uniform draped over the chair at the foot of his bed. He swung his feet to the floor and pulled his hand away from his side. The small, circular scar left by the slug from the bearded man's gun was framed in a rectangle of light streaming in from the half-open bathroom door.

He traced the outline of the scar with his finger. The bullet had passed through his side, banked off the cash register on the counter behind him, and entered Billy Hotard's chest, killing him instantly. The bearded man had lingered a bit longer, gurgling and clawing at his throat, where the bullet from Carter's automatic had disintegrated his jugular.

Carter got up, walked into the bathroom, and let his eyes

adjust to the light while he urinated. Flushing the toilet, he moved to the sink and splashed cold water on his face. He had just turned twenty-six, but the reflection staring back at him from the mirror above the sink could have been that of a man ten years his senior. The skin around his pale green eyes had begun to wrinkle, and the light brown tangle atop his head was run through with prematurely graying strands.

Walking back into his room, Carter stared at a framed newspaper clipping that hung on the wall above his chest of drawers. The clipping's headline read LOCAL COP KILLS PENAL FARM ESCAPEE.

He moved to the window and stared out at the quiet street. It would be several hours before the tiny south-Texas town began waking up. He lay on the bed and began searching for familiar faces amid the swirls of the plaster ceiling.

Finding none, he rolled over onto his side. "Things always look better in the morning," he mumbled into his pillow.

TWO

FLIES ON RICE

Skeeter Tipson sat at his desk in the booking area of the Bottleneck Police Department, sucking the cream filling from a pastry he had found while cleaning out his filing cabinet. Sergeant Matt Goolsby leaned against the desk, watching him.

"How long's that thing been in there?" Goolsby asked.

"Can't be more than a month," Skeeter mumbled through a mouthful of cream. "Doc Barlow made me quit eating them."

"After you had that fit?"

"Yeah."

Skeeter took another pull from the pastry and tossed it into the wastebasket beside his desk. "You gonna let Toke out?"

"Might as well," Goolsby said. "He ought to be good and sobered up by now."

Goolsby walked around the desk and down the hall that led to the holding cells, while Skeeter opened one of his desk drawers and took out a small, tattered cardboard box.

Carter walked into the station as Goolsby was escorting Toke Wheeler to Skeeter's desk. He stopped just inside the door, took a cigarette from the pack in his shirt pocket, and lit it, tossing the match into a potted plant a few feet away.

He looked Toke over. The muscular stump of a torso was wrapped in a grubby T-shirt that bore the logo of Arty's Quick Lube, the garage Toke had owned since winning it from Arty Gilrod in a drunken card game several months earlier. Toke's jeans were stained with oil and grease, and his heavy leather workboots were beginning to break apart at the seams.

Skeeter pushed the box across the desk toward Toke and handed him a clipboard. "Sign at the bottom for your stuff."

Toke took the clipboard and scrawled his name across the bottom of the attached form. His right forearm had bulged to half again the size of his left from the months of turning wrenches at the garage. He tossed the clipboard onto the desk and took a piece of chewing gum and a wristwatch from the box.

He slipped the watch on. "It's broke."

"Then it was broken when you came in here," Goolsby said.

"I don't see why you boys don't spend your time catching some real criminals," Toke said, unwrapping the gum and stuffing it into his mouth.

"You're the worst thing we've got going right now, Toke," Skeeter said. "You know that."

"All I know is, every time I take a drink, you're on me like flies on rice," Toke said, "and that shit ain't right."

Toke blew a huge bubble as he turned to leave. Carter held the door open for him, watched him walk through, and tossed the remainder of his cigarette out after him. He walked over to Skeeter's desk.

"What was he in for this time?"

"He was out in old Ben Gooding's corn field last night," Skeeter said, "running around and screaming at the top of his lungs."

Goolsby grinned. "Yeah, he told me there was a pair of overalls with nobody in them chasing him around town. He was trying to lose them in the corn."

Carter picked up the clipboard that held that morning's duty roster. He began searching for his name and assignment.

"It ain't on there," Skeeter said.

"Why not?"

"The chief told me to leave it off. He wants to see you in his office, and he's got that shrink from over in Braintree with him."

"Great," Carter said, handing the clipboard back to Skeeter.

Chief Franklin Dykes filled a styrofoam cup with lukewarm coffee and turned to Dr. David Fritch, who was sitting in a chair next to the cramped office's only window.

"Coffee?"

"No thanks," Fritch said, not looking up from the manila folder spread open on his lap. He took out a handkerchief and coughed into it.

Dykes put the coffee pot back on its base and walked over to his desk.

"Not surprising, really," Fritch said.

"What?"

"It's not surprising that your officer is still having problems," Fritch said, "considering what happened."

"He'd only been on the force a few months."

"And most of that time was spent handing out traffic tickets and arresting people he's known since high school. Then there's this business with the vest."

Dykes nodded. "He thinks that if he'd been wearing it, Hotard would still be alive."

"He's probably right."

"Hell, we'd only had the things a week. Nobody was wearing them. You ever wear one? They're damned uncomfortable."

"Where'd they find Carter's again?"

"On the front seat of his patrol car."

There was a knock at the door. "Come in," Dykes said, sitting down.

Carter entered the office. "You wanted to see me, Chief?"

"Have a seat, Carter," Dykes said, motioning toward a chair in front of his desk.

Carter sat down. "How ya been, Doc?"

Fritch snapped the file shut and looked up at Carter. "I'm doing fine. How about you?"

"No complaints."

"The doc here's a little worried about you," Dykes said.

"Oh?"

"How have you been sleeping since we talked last, Carter?" Fritch asked.

"Well enough."

"Any dreams?"

"Last night I dreamed my grandma came looking for me at suppertime and found me with a hooker. Does that mean anything?"

Dykes laughed, spilling a bit of coffee on his shirt. He dabbed at the stain with his tie. "I think he means are you still having nightmares about, y'know, the thing out at Hotard's."

"Yeah."

Fritch nodded gravely.

"Maybe you should take some time off," Dykes said.

"Why?"

"Just a few days," Fritch said. "Take a vacation. Relax. When you get back, you can call my secretary and set up a regular appointment schedule."

"For what?"

"Counseling. I want you to come in and see me at least twice a month. I think you're having a delayed stress reaction to what you went through."

"You came up with that without showing me a single inkblot, Doc? I wanna look at some inkblots. Right now."

"Nobody's saying you're crazy, Carter," Dykes said.

"Not at all," Fritch added. "This isn't uncommon for someone who's been through a highly stressful experience. It happens all the time to cops, firemen, soldiers under fire."

Carter sighed. "So you think this is a good idea, Chief?"

"Leave this afternoon. Go visit your relatives. I'm sure they'd be happy to see you. When you come back, we'll find some work for you to do around the station until you get this ironed out."

Carter got up from his chair and left the room, avoiding Fritch's gaze.

Fritch stuffed Carter's file into his briefcase. "There now, that wasn't so difficult. He'll probably enjoy the time off, don't you think?"

Dykes rolled his eyes.

THREE

THE PERFECT COMBINATION

Del Mooney and Jimmy Pope sat across from each other at a rickety card table next to the window in Ben Yelverton's Pawn Shop playing chess. The game had been going on for over three hours.

"It's still your move," Del said.

"I know," Jimmy said. "Don't rush me." He studied the board for a few seconds before moving one of his rooks to capture Del's remaining knight.

"Good one," Del said, hunching over the board. He and Jimmy had been staring across the card table at each other every morning since they had both retired from their jobs at the Bottleneck public works department on the same day a year earlier.

Their co-workers had chipped in and bought them a set of checkers with which to pass their retirement, and Ben Yelverton, who was Del's second cousin, suggested that the two play in his shop. It was, after all, a neutral playing field, where neither combatant would have an advantage.

Yelverton's suggestion hadn't been completely selfless. He loved the idea of having a couple of crusty old men playing checkers and sniping at each other in the window of his place. He figured he could even charge his customers a little extra for the ambience Del and Jimmy created.

Despite Ben's promise of an even playing field, Jimmy had quickly come to dominate the games. The old men were lifelong friends, and like most old friendships, theirs had an element of competitiveness to it. The constant losing soon began to wear on Del, and after coming across a volume on chess strategies at a Corpus Christi bookstore, he had suggested that they switch games.

Jimmy agreed, and with the book on his side, Del had wiped the board with him for the first few weeks. Jimmy, however, had begun to catch on to the nuances of the game, and Del could now see himself in serious danger of beginning a new losing streak. He leaned forward, and a bead of sweat fell from his forehead onto one of the few pawns still in play.

Jimmy watched Del struggling over the game and grinned. He looked out the window at the Wells Fargo armored car parked in front of the bank across the street. It had pulled up fifteen minutes ago, and the driver had gone inside, leaving his partner milling around on the sidewalk in front of the bank.

Carter entered the pawn shop carrying a Browning automatic shotgun. He saw Del and Jimmy and walked over to the table. "How's it going, boys?"

"It'll be going all right if he hurries up and moves," Jimmy said.

"Fuck it," Del muttered, placing his finger lightly on one of his pawns and moving it a space to the left. "I give up." He leaned back in his chair and studied Carter's shotgun.

"Nice shotgun."

"Thanks," Carter said. "Thought I might pawn it for a little travelling money."

"Going on a trip?" Jimmy asked.

"Yeah, I've got some vacation time coming."

Jimmy nodded, only half interested in Carter's reply. He was watching the armored car. The driver had come out of the bank carrying some sort of document, which he now folded carefully and stuffed into his shirt pocket. He signaled to his partner, and the two of them walked around to the back of the truck. The driver took a set of keys from his pocket and unlocked the truck's rear door, swinging it open. He and his partner reached inside, and each withdrew a large canvas bag with leather straps for handles. The bags were bulging.

"Check this out," Jimmy said as the two lugged their charges toward the bank's front door. Carter and Del now watched with him.

"Hey, Carter," Del said, "let me borrow your shotgun a minute. I need to walk over and make a withdrawal."

The three of them chuckled as the men across the street disappeared inside the bank.

Jimmy turned his attention from the window back to the chess game and studied Del's move. "Wouldn't need a shotgun," he said.

"What?" Del asked.

"Wouldn't need a shotgun to make a withdrawal from that bank. Wouldn't need no stethoscope to crack the safe neither."

"What are you talking about, Jimmy?" Carter asked, grinning a little at the old man's suddenly serious tone of voice.

"You two remember my niece, Berta Dobbs?"

Carter and Del nodded.

"She worked over there for old man Rickster as a teller for

a little while, right after she got out of college. Stayed there about a year. She finally had to quit on account of he brought in his daughter to manage the place, and Berta said she'd be damned if she'd work for the boss's daughter."

"Which daughter?" Carter asked. "He's got two."

"The oldest one, I think. Cindy or something. I forget her name."

"Mindy," Carter said.

"Well, anyway, the week before Berta left, the girl changed the big safe's combination. Said she needed it to be something she could remember better. That same day, Berta was nosing through some tax forms, and guess what?"

"What?" Del asked.

"She saw the girl's birthday, and damned if she hadn't changed the combination to her birthday. The girl wasn't any too bright."

"So, what was it?" Del asked.

"What was what?"

"The girl's birthday."

"Hell, I don't remember. Why?"

Del leaned forward in his chair to answer, but Carter put a hand on his shoulder. "This conversation's gone far enough," he said, smiling. "I'd hate like hell to have to lock you two up."

The sound of a toilet flushing could be heard from the back of the store. A few seconds later, Ben Yelverton pushed his way through a beaded curtain behind the shop's counter.

"What's going on over there?" he asked. "An assholes convention?"

"Just planning a robbery, Ben," Carter said. He walked over to the counter and placed his shotgun down on it.

"Pawning or selling?" Ben asked, eyeing the gun. "I'm easy."

FOUR

PARTS UNKNOWN

C arter pulled up to his Aunt Enid's place just as the sun
was beginning to set. It painted the clouds a pastel
orange that reminded him of fiberglass attic insulation.

Enid's son Cliff sat on the porch sipping a beer. He watched
Carter get out of his truck and take his suitcase from behind
the seat.

"Howdy, stranger," Cliff said.

Carter stepped up onto the porch. "How's it going, Cliff?"

"Not too bad."

"Where's Enid?"

"She's playing bingo at the church tonight."

"Got one of those for me?"

Cliff reached into the small cooler beside his chair and
pulled out a beer. He handed it to Carter.

Carter cracked the can and took a long drink. "I was thinking about riding out to Uncle Lonnie's for a while. Wanna
go?"

"You'll have plenty of time for visiting tomorrow," Cliff

said. "I've got plans for us tonight. Go put your stuff in the house and we'll get going."

~

Carter and Cliff sat in folding chairs, three rows away from the makeshift ring that had been erected in the Saltlick High School gymnasium. They were watching two fat, spandex-clad midgets bounce each other off the canvas. The elderly man refereeing the match was trying desperately to mask his boredom.

"I hate the midgets," Cliff said, taking a bite from his corndog. "They're fun to watch for the first few minutes, but after that it's just a freak show, y'know?"

"Yeah," Carter chuckled. "I feel the same way."

Carter looked around the gymnasium. There were about thirty people seated in the chairs around the ring and in the bleachers. A pretty impressive turnout, Carter thought, considering the population of Saltlick was only about two hundred.

One of the midgets finally pinned the other for the required three count.

"'Bout fucking time," Cliff said. "I was getting ready to go up there and kick their little asses myself."

A thin, balding man wearing a plaid sports coat climbed into the ring and stood beside the referee. He held a mega-phone in one hand and a grimy index card in the other.

"And now your main event," he read from the card. "Fight-ing from the blue corner, and weighing in at two hundred and forty pounds . . . Saltlick's own Crusher Collins!"

Crusher Collins came running from beneath the bleachers to Carter's right and jumped into the ring. His huge belly flopped grotesquely over the waistband of his leopard-skin tights. A few people near the top of the bleachers, doubtless Crusher's relatives, clapped weakly.

"And now, fighting from the red corner," the plaid man bellowed, "hailing from parts unknown . . . Luscious Johnny Famine!"

Famine got a cooler reception as he bounded from beneath the bleachers to Carter's left and propelled his gawky, emaciated frame into the ring. He was at least six and a half feet tall and had on black tights and a silver and black sequined mask.

The plaid man scurried out of the ring as if avoiding an oncoming train. He sat down at the scorer's table in front of a large bell and rang it. The wrestlers circled each other in the middle of the ring before locking arms. Carter looked at his watch, careful not to let Cliff see him.

Five minutes into the match, Luscious Johnny Famine was already in dire trouble, with Crusher tossing him around the ring like a rag doll.

Crusher grinned broadly as he applied a sinister-looking hold to his opponent's neck.

"It's all over now," Cliff muttered.

Within a few seconds, Famine had been reduced to a limp wreck. The referee lifted his hand, held it for a moment, then let it drop heavily to the canvas.

The announcer rang the bell and jumped into the ring as Crusher released the ruined thing that had been his adversary and raised his hands in triumph.

"Your winner!" he proclaimed, gesturing grandly toward the preening Crusher.

Crusher brushed past the referee and announcer and knelt beside his fallen opponent, grabbing a handful of mask. He looked around the gymnasium expectantly, but no one seemed particularly interested in Luscious Johnny Famine's true identity.

He pulled the mask off anyway. To Carter's surprise, a few gasps of what seemed to be genuine amazement could be heard from the crowd. Cliff snorted disgustedly.

"Bip Carson," he said, shaking his head in disappointment.

"What?" Carter asked.

Cliff stood up. "Parts unknown my ass!" he screamed at the ring. "That boy bags groceries at the A&P! Name's Bip!"

The ring announcer looked at Cliff and shrugged. Carter grabbed Cliff and managed to pull him back into his seat.

Crusher swung the mask around for a minute, like a Greek warrior who had just beheaded a Gorgon that was tormenting his village. He then took a windup and hurled it from the ring.

The mask landed in an empty seat in front of Carter. He picked it up and stuffed it into his jacket pocket, then stood up.

"Souvenir, huh?" Cliff said.

"Yeah. Let's get the hell out of here before the crowd riots."

FIVE

UNCLE LONNIE

Carter woke to the smell of frying bacon. He rolled off the couch and walked into the kitchen, where Enid stood at the stove preparing breakfast. He kissed her on the cheek and sat down at the table.

"How was bingo?" he asked.

"What?" Enid took a plate of scrambled eggs from the counter, added a few strips of bacon, and placed it on the table in front of Carter.

"Cliff told me you were playing bingo at the church."

"You know I don't gamble, Carter."

Cliff walked into the kitchen. Enid eyed him accusingly as he walked to the counter and began piling eggs onto a plate.

"What?" Cliff asked, withering beneath her stare.

"Why'd you tell him I was playing bingo at the church, boy? Has it gotten so that it's easier for you to lie than tell the truth?"

"You know that ain't fair, Ma. I just didn't want him to worry."

Carter nibbled at his bacon. "Worry about what, Cliff?"

"Talk to her about it," Cliff said. "I'm late for work." He shoveled a spoonful of eggs into his mouth and walked out.

"That boy's gonna kill me, Carter," Enid said. "He's got his daddy's temper, and it was temper that killed his daddy. You know it's true."

Carter nodded. Enid's late husband, Dexter, had died of a massive coronary after arguing with an exterminator over the rate at which termites reproduce. "Where'd you go last night?"

"I took your Uncle Lonnie to see a doctor in Houston. A nervologist."

Carter dropped the piece of bacon he had been gnawing onto his plate. His Uncle Lonnie, who was Enid's brother, had raised him after his parents were killed in a car accident when he was nine years old. "What's wrong with him?"

"The doctor said he's got some kind of degenerative thing," Enid said. She sat across the table from Carter. "It's like old-timer's, but it works on you faster. He won't be able to take care of himself much longer."

"Enid, I talked to Lonnie not two weeks ago. He sounded fine."

"He's in and out. He was okay when you talked to him, but if you'd called back half an hour later, he might not have been able to tell you his own name. I know it's hard to believe, but it's that bad."

"What's going to happen to him?"

"I don't know. I wish to God I could take care of him myself, but I can't. At night it wouldn't be a problem, but I'm working all day, and so is Cliff. I practically had to beg to get yesterday and today off from the plant, and Cliff's in the same boat."

"And somebody's gonna have to be with him all the time?"

"That's what the doctor said. He'll require 'constant care' to make sure he doesn't hurt himself."

Carter got up from the table. He took a carton of orange juice from the refrigerator and drank straight from it, straining the juice through his teeth and chewing the tiny bits of pulp.

"Please drink the juice out of a glass, Carter," Enid sighed. "You know I love you, honey, but that's just plain disgusting."

Carter took a small glass from the cabinet and half filled it. "We'll have to put him into some kind of home, I guess."

"There's a place up there that the doctor said is good with cases like Lonnie's. The only problem is the cost. This place is what they call cheap, but it's way out of our range."

"Maybe if we all pitched in."

"Still too much."

Carter sat down. He reached across the table and took Enid's hand. "It's all right. We'll figure something out."

"Y'know, Lonnie always took care of me when we were kids, and even later, any time I had trouble, I could go to him. Now he needs somebody to take care of him, and there's nothing I can do about it."

Enid began crying, and Carter felt his insides knot up. To say Lonnie had always been there for him too would have been an understatement, so he just kept his mouth shut and tried to think.

SIX

SMOKE SIGNALS

Jimmy Dale Gilmore's "Nothing of the Kind" was playing on the radio as Carter crossed the Mingo County Line. He was driving along a stretch of county two-lane that was bordered on either side by cotton fields. The rows of cotton stretched away from the road like the remnants of a dirty cloud that had wafted to the earth through a cheese grater.

Carter and Enid had driven out to Lonnie's place that morning after breakfast and found him sitting on a tree stump at the edge of the small pond behind his house. He was holding a cane pole between his legs and staring blankly at a green dragonfly perched halfway up it.

Lonnie had remained motionless when Carter spoke to him, not looking up until a small bass broke the water near the bank and frightened the dragonfly away.

They had talked for a while, mostly about the rotten fishing and the weather. Lonnie seemed fine, and Carter was beginning to think Enid had exaggerated the extent of his illness until he pulled his hook from the water and showed the two of them the threadbare sock he had been using for bait.

"No wonder the fish aren't biting," Carter had said as Enid sobbed quietly.

The DJ segued into Billy Joe Shaver's "Georgia on a Fast Train." Carter heard a low buzzing. He adjusted the radio, thinking maybe he was picking up some sort of interference from the power lines paralleling the road.

The buzzing became louder. Looking up from the radio, Carter spied its source. A small, single-engine plane was spiralling skyward above the field to his right, about a quarter of a mile ahead of him.

The plane was climbing toward the words "YOU SAVE BIG!" which hung suspended in smoky letters against the perfect blue sky. As it neared them, the plane turned sharply in the direction of the road and began trailing a thick stream of smoke, underlining the wisping phrase.

The stream didn't stop as the plane went into a severe dive, at the foot of which it flew across the road just in front of Carter's truck.

Carter drove into the cloud and lost the road. He toed the brake gently at first, thinking he had fifty yards or so until the road curved sharply to the right.

He didn't realize that he'd misjudged the distance until he felt the truck bounce across the ditch. He stood on the brake, but it was too late.

Carter heard the sound of twisting metal as he was thrown forward. His head cracked against the windshield, and everything went black.

≈

Carter lay on a cracked leather sofa next to a cluttered desk at one end of a small hangar, his eyes fluttering as he struggled back to consciousness. He sat up, wincing as he fingered the lump on his forehead.

Through the hangar's partially open door, he could see Toke Wheeler standing beside his tow truck and talking to an auburn-haired woman and a slightly overweight man who were both wearing blue coveralls.

After a minute or so, Toke scratched his armpit and hopped into his truck. He started it and drove out of sight.

Carter stood up slowly and hobbled around the desk, sitting down heavily in the high-backed leather chair behind it. He looked around the desk. On it were several appointment books, a framed picture of a young boy, and a stack of business cards. He reached for one of the cards. It read VENUS SKYWRITING.

Carter slipped the card into his shirt pocket and reached for the picture. The boy, who looked to be nine or ten years old, was wearing some sort of uniform, with a multicolored crest on the pocket and a braided yellow rope hanging from the shoulder.

Carter's head began to throb and his vision blurred. He dropped the picture onto the desk and put his hands to his face.

"You all right?" came a voice from the direction of the hangar door. Carter pulled his hands away from his face and ogled the woman he had seen outside with Toke and the other man.

Her coveralls were unzipped in front. The white T-shirt she wore under them stopped several inches short of her waist. Carter tried to focus on her bellybutton as she walked over.

"Hey, maybe you'd better get back on the couch," the woman said.

"You must be Venus."

The woman laughed. "Not quite. My name's Dakota Winslow. This is my place."

"You the one strafing the road?"

"Yeah, sorry about that," she said, rubbing her nose. "I lost control for a minute."

"Who's gonna 'save big,' anyway? The boll weevils?"

"No, I've got a job coming up over a used car dealership. I was just trying to get some practice in. Is your head all right?"

Carter touched the lump again. "I guess so. You call an ambulance or anything?"

"My mechanic, Horace, checked you out. He used to be a medic in the army."

Horace walked into the hangar. "That guy's got the truck out of the ditch," he said.

"Is that Toke Wheeler out there?" Carter asked.

"I think that's his name," Dakota said. "You know him?"

"I've arrested him," Carter said groggily, leaning back in the chair.

"You're a cop?" Horace asked, placing his hands on his hips and taking a step back. He shot Dakota a nervous glance, which she dismissed with a wave.

Toke entered the hangar. "He riding back with me?" he said, gesturing toward Carter.

"I think he ought to rest a while longer," Dakota said.

Toke eyed Carter more closely. A look of recognition spread across his face. "Well, why don't you just drop him off at the garage when he's up to travelling. I need to get on back to town."

Toke turned and left the hangar, followed by Horace.

Dakota walked over to Carter and took him gently by the arm.

"Lie down on the couch a while," she said, helping him to his feet. "I'll give you a ride back to town when you feel like moving."

"All right," Carter said, walking over to the couch and sitting down gingerly. "I hope you drive better than you fly."

SEVEN

WHEELS

Carter's truck was suspended above the floor of Toke's garage on a hydraulic rack. Toke sat on the front seat of the truck, drinking an Old Milwaukee and thinking about his trip out to the airstrip that afternoon.

Toke hated cops, and normally he would have gotten a big kick out of telling Carter to fix his own damn truck. But business had been bad since Arty Gilrod's suicide two weeks earlier. Toke had won the garage from Arty, whose grandfather had established it in 1949, in a liquor-soaked poker game.

Arty had always done a booming business. Toke thought he had finally hit the jackpot when he woke up the morning after the game the owner of Bottleneck's busiest repair shop. He decided to keep the name Arty's Quick Lube for the sake of Arty's regular customers.

Word got around about the card game, however, and most of the town blamed Toke for the likeable Arty's subsequent and rapid descent into drunken self-pity and depression.

After losing the family business, Arty had only ventured from the apartment he rented above the garage of elderly Delia Lodish to purchase the rum and cheese doodles that sustained him during the last weeks of his life.

When he failed to stagger down the stairs one morning, Mrs. Lodish investigated. She found Arty sprawled on his bathroom floor with an empty bottle of prescription medication clutched in his hand and a vile green foam hardening on his lips. The shock was too much for Mrs. Lodish. She suffered a heart attack and died instantly.

Arty and Mrs. Lodish were buried at opposite ends of the Lone Tree Cemetery on the morning and afternoon of the same day. Both of the funerals were heavily attended. Arty had been very popular, and Mrs. Lodish, a retired teacher, had taught half the town long division.

After the dual outpourings of grief, business at the garage had tapered off quickly. Toke couldn't understand it. He had won the place fair and square and was just as good a mechanic as Arty had been, maybe better.

The call from the Winslow woman had come as a godsend. He could gouge the cop for repairs and meet his mortgage payment for at least another month while he decided on whether or not to torch the place for the insurance.

Toke finished the beer and tossed the can out the truck's open window onto a heap of rubbish next to his tool cabinet. He looked around the inside of the truck. He took his arm off the center console and opened it. There was a holstered pistol and some loose change inside. Toke scooped up the change and dropped it into his breast pocket, then picked up the pistol and took it from its holster.

He put the gun back into the console and closed the lid, then leaned over and opened the glove compartment. A balled-up piece of sequined cloth fell out. He picked it up and pulled it into shape.

Slipping Luscious Johnny Famine's mask over his hand, Toke put his thumb and pinky through the large eyeholes, wiggling them. He grunted, pulled the mask from his hand, and shoved it back where he had found it.

Slamming the glove compartment shut, Toke jumped down from the truck. He walked over to his ice chest and took out another beer. He cracked it open and was slurping at the foam when he heard a knock on one of the garage's massive sliding doors.

Toke walked over and stood by the door, sipping his beer until the knock came again. "Closed," he growled. "Come back tomorrow."

"Open up, Wheeler," Carter called from the other side of the door.

Toke opened the door and let Carter in. "Where's Pancho Barnes? I'm surprised she ain't sticking around you a while to make sure your head ain't broke."

"She took off."

"You've got one hell of a lawsuit against that bitch, you know it?"

"It's just a bump on the head."

"You ought to get a lawyer, son. That's what I'd do. A head can only take so many bumps, and you're one good one closer to the squirrel farm now."

"I'll be careful," Carter said, walking over to the hydraulic rack and looking at his truck's mangled undercarriage. "How's my truck?"

"Not good. The axle's broke."

"Shit," Carter mumbled, climbing up into the cab and taking his gun from the console. He opened the glove compartment and the mask fell out. He stuffed it into his pocket.

"Be at least a week," Toke said. "I gotta order parts for it. You can use the loaner."

"Loaner?"

Carter followed Toke outside to the back of the garage, where an old Thunderbird with rusted fenders and four bald tires was parked in a sea of weeds. Toke handed him the keys. "Rides so good you'll have to get out and let your ass laugh every couple of miles," he said, grinning toothily.

EIGHT

A FOGGY NOTION

That night, Carter dreamed about Billy Hotard. In his dream, he and Billy were being ushered into a bright red Ferris wheel carriage by a tall, black carnival worker wearing a tuxedo jacket over his grubby jeans and T-shirt.

When Carter and Billy were seated in the carriage, the carny turned to a set of levers that were jutting from a rusty metal gearbox and pulled one with a fluorescent yellow handle.

The carriage rose. Carter looked around and saw that the ride had been set up in the middle of Bottleneck's War Memorial Park. He could see the station in the distance, and across the street from it the city garage. Jimbo Spell was milling about aimlessly in front of the garage, his hands shoved into his pockets.

When the carriage reached its highest point, the Ferris wheel stopped suddenly. Billy turned to Carter and said, "What's eating you?"

"You ever meet my Uncle Lonnie?"

"From over in Saltlick?"

"Yeah."

"I met him once. We were both entered in a fishing tournament at Lake Roosevelt. They disqualified me for using dynamite, but I seem to recall him placing second or third."

Carter nodded. "He raised me after my parents died, taught me everything I know. Now he can hardly tie his own shoes."

"That's too bad," Billy said, his voice trailing off as he watched a cluster of scantily clad women frolicking at the edge of the park's small lake.

"Where'd they come from?" Carter asked, looking down at the women.

"How should I know? It's your dream."

"Oh yeah."

"So what's wrong with your uncle? He get kicked in the head by a mule?"

"It's his head, but the doctors say it's some kind of degenerative thing."

"You mean his head's shrinking?"

"No, he just ain't thinking right, that's all. The worst thing about it is, nobody in my family can afford to put him in a place that can take care of him."

"Some kind of home?"

"Yeah."

Billy leaned back in the carriage and spit over the side.

"Why are you telling me this, Carter?"

"I don't know. I guess I thought we kind of shared something."

"Because you got me killed?"

"You really believe that, Billy?"

Billy shrugged. "Don't really matter what I believe now."

Carter heard a low buzzing. He looked to his left and saw

a small plane flying over the town's main street. It swooped low and buzzed the downtown area, then banked and flew toward the Ferris wheel. It passed by about fifty yards away, and Carter could see Dakota Winslow in the cockpit. He felt Billy tugging at his arm.

"What?" he asked irritably as the plane flew behind a low-hanging bank of clouds.

"Do you remember Mindy Rickster's birthday?" Billy whispered, his eyes darting about nervously as if he thought someone might be eavesdropping on them.

"Why?"

"Just curious. I know you took her out on her birthday when you were both in high school. You stopped at my store that night and tried to buy beer with a fake ID, remember?"

"Yeah, I do. You took my ID and called Mindy's old man the next day. He made her stop seeing me after that."

"So you never got in her pants?"

"No."

"Hope there aren't any hard feelings."

"I was a lot more upset about the ID. I gave twenty bucks for it."

"You got ripped off," Billy giggled. "So do you remember her birthday or not?"

"Sure I do. March thirteenth. Day after mine."

"Then sure as you were born, your problems are solved."

As Carter thought about this, the flesh between the index and middle fingers of his right hand began to itch. The itch became a burn. He rubbed frantically at the burning with his left hand and woke with a start, jumping up from the couch and flinging the mangled cigarette into the fireplace.

He sat back down and rubbed at the blister that was beginning to rise between his fingers. He reached to get another cigarette, but the pack on the coffee table was empty.

"Shit," he grumbled, looking at his watch. Most of Bottle-neck's convenience stores would be closing soon. He got up and grabbed his jacket from the back of the chair he had been using as a foot rest while he slept.

He could hear the keys to the loaner jingling in his pocket as he slipped the jacket on and walked out the door.

NINE

BEER GOGGLES

On Friday nights, Stu Pateman usually slipped on his beer goggles at around seven o'clock with the help of a six-pack of whatever beer was on sale at the Sip and Save near his house.

After a few hours of solitary drinking, he would meet up with his friends from the rendering plant, and they would drive out to Shy Anne's, a popular roadhouse. There they would all move on to the harder stuff.

Shy Anne's always had a country and western band play-ing on Friday nights, and thanks to the bar's proximity to an all girls community college a few miles up the highway, there was never any shortage of dancing partners.

Most of the girls who spent their Friday nights at Shy Anne's were of the homely sort, mousy girls who were drunk with the heady freedom of being away from home and out from under their parents' thumbs for the first time.

Stu didn't mind that the girls weren't beauty queens. Though he was by most standards a fairly handsome man, he had never danced with—or done anything else with—a really attractive woman. This had mainly to do with his natural shyness, which he tried desperately to overcome by prodigious alcohol consumption.

The spirits also helped to overcome any deficiencies on his dancing partners' end. They all looked great through his beer goggles.

This night, with its boozing and dancing, had been like any other Friday night, until Stu's friend Carl began spouting off about some insanity he had read in one of the supermarket tabloids he always carried into the bathroom with him at work.

Stu usually found Carl's drunken ramblings amusing, no matter what they were about, but for some reason this monologue rubbed him the wrong way. Maybe it was the rapt gaze that his partner for the evening—for once a real looker—fixed on Carl whenever his mouth started moving.

Carl had wholeheartedly adopted a theory he had gleaned from one of the tabloids and was expounding on it for anyone willing to listen. He apparently believed that the government was employing a team of psychics to read the mind of a captured bigfoot they believed to be a Martian spy.

Stu countered him on every point while throwing back shots of Jack Daniel's. He felt like an idiot the whole time, but he couldn't stop himself—at least not until Carl leaned across the table and socked him squarely on the chin. Stu flew backwards and landed in a heap. He was struggling to his feet when a phalanx of bouncers pounced upon him and Carl and began dragging them toward the door.

Stu's buddies were so put out with him that they refused to give him a lift home, so he hitched a ride with a pulpwood cutter who was leaving the roadhouse at the same time he and Carl were being thrown out. The logger, whose name was Stan, was missing two fingers on his left hand and three on his right. His clawlike appendages, combined with a slight sunburn, gave Stan the appearance of a giant, fleshy crab.

Stu muttered something to this effect. Stan stood on the brakes and shoved him roughly from the cab of the truck, then sped away in a cloud of wood chips and sawdust. Stu was standing at the south end of Lassiter Street, Bottleneck's main drag, with a six-mile walk back to his house. He brushed himself off and got started, weaving down the middle of the road.

Fifteen minutes later, he wasn't making very good time. The whiskey and violence had left his beer goggles considerably fogged. Stu had just finished vomiting down a storm drain when the sound of breaking glass from up the street peaked his curiosity.

He walked as quickly as he safely could until he was standing in front of a pawn shop across the street from the bank. Hearing the sound of glass grinding under heavy shoes, he stealthily sank into the pawn shop's recessed doorway.

After a minute or so, he saw a tall, thin man wearing a leather jacket and what looked like a sequined ski mask emerge from a broken window at the side of the bank. In his right hand, the masked man was carrying a large canvas bag. He looked around furtively, then walked quickly down the alley that ran between the bank and Crowley's General Store.

Stu started across the street. When he reached the mouth of the alley, he heard the slamming of a car door, followed by an engine on its last legs being prodded to life.

Stu's strength was gone. He looked around, and seeing that he was alone in the alley, found a comfortable spot to spend the rest of the night.

TEN

DINO'S PLACE

With a population of 4,269, Bottleneck, Texas, was Mingo County's largest town. It had been founded in 1848 by Dino Bonebrite, a disreputable city councilman from Minnesota who left his wife and family for a life of frontier abandonment after receiving a fat bribe from the owner of a brothel he frequented.

Dino used his graft to fund the construction of a trading post and saloon, around which a bustling community comprised predominately of gamblers and whoremongers soon sprang up. He dubbed the town Bottleneck, because the plain upon which he had built his trading post tapered to a narrow strip of land running between the bends in two curving rivers. The slim earthen bridge led to a lush, green plain used as a grazing stop by cattlemen. They would drive their longhorns through the bottleneck between the muddy channels, then sample the town's tawdry wares in shifts.

Bottleneck's early existence depended heavily upon the inhabitants' good relations with the native Caddo Indians, who considered the valley Dino had chosen for the site of his trading post their own. The Caddo weren't thrilled with the rapid influx of rowdy whites, and Dino was constantly forced to use his politician's wiles in smoothing over rubs and quelling the fears of the Caddo's tribal elders.

Dino smoked his last peace pipe in 1889 after a cowboy visiting Bottleneck got drunk, galloped into a nearby Caddo encampment, and collapsed in the entranceway of the chief's tepee. The unfortunate cowboy was immediately skinned alive, but Dino managed to save the town from massacre through a night of bourbon-laced negotiations with the chief.

At sunrise, Dino staggered back to town, where he fell down a well and drowned after being beaten savagely about the head and shoulders with a live chicken by a Mexican girl he had been promising to marry for over a month. No one in town was willing to fish Dino's corpse from the bottom of the well, so it was decided to entomb him by sealing it.

Dino was gone, but Bottleneck crept slowly onward, its population gradually swelling from hundreds to thousands, and its makeup shifting from one of miscreants to one made up mostly of the more community-minded elements of its early citizenry.

Every other decade or so a group of spinsters and widows calling themselves a historic preservation society would organize and clamor for the restoration and upkeep of Dino's trading post, citing its priceless value to posterity. They'd slap a fresh coat of paint over the shabby little building's rotting boards and pat themselves on the back for having prolonged the life of the one-time den of debauchery.

The center of the town's activities gradually drifted away from the area of the trading post, however, and it had been some thirty years since the last bunch of bored and concerned citizens felt charitable toward the town's founder or his rotting monument. The trading post was left largely forgotten on the town's fringes, the sound of its saloon doors creaking as they were blown in the wind the lone reminder of Bottleneck's fast-track beginnings.

It was to this sound that Carter woke. He was lying in the back seat of the loaner, surrounded by crushed beer cans, clutching the leather handle of the canvas moneybag he had spirited away from the bank. He sat up and pulled the bag from the floorboard to his lap, opening it. He reached inside and pulled out a bound stack of hundreds. Peering into the bag, he saw what appeared to be at least twenty more just like the one in his hand. He shoved the stack into the inside pocket of his jacket and climbed out of the car.

He had parked alongside the dirt road running in front of what was left of the trading post. He slammed the car door shut and walked toward the building, carrying the bag of money. Inside, he tossed the bag onto the dirt floor and looked around for something to dig with. He found a slat of wood in the corner and began making a hole near a long, caved-in structure that had once been a bar. Once the hole was deep enough, he took the mask from his pocket, shoved it into the bag, and tossed the bundle in.

He covered the items, smoothed over the disrupted ground, and marked the spot with an old paint can he found behind the bar. His hands shaking, he took a cigarette from his pocket and lit it, then walked out into the morning sun.

ELEVEN

FINE LINES

A t home, Carter made a pot of coffee and drank the first cup black while he sat at the kitchen table staring at the stack of hundreds. He had placed the money on a ceramic plate, as if it would burn through the table if there weren't some sort of heat-resistant buffer beneath it.

When he finished his coffee, he got up and poured himself another cup, adding cream and sugar this time. He sipped it as he paced around the kitchen, thinking back on a story Cliff had told him several years earlier.

They had been driving to Houston to watch an Astros game when Cliff launched into a monologue about his friend Tiny Jeffers. Tiny had been a portly man when he and Cliff first began working together on the assembly line at the Swinson Aircraft plant in Saltlick. Tiny wore a thin mustache, and at his chubbiest, he bore a striking resemblance to Grand Ole Opry mainstay Ricky Skaggs, so much so that Cliff and many other co-workers had taken to calling him "Bluegrass."

Not liking the nickname, Tiny had gone on a diet; but he was cursed, for when he reached his goal weight, he looked remarkably like Adolph Hitler. This gave rise to a whole new series of nicknames and jibes, that were much more sinister and mean spirited.

Cliff said that Tiny's metamorphosis was a good example of the fine lines walked by many men. "Hell, if it ain't but forty pounds from Ricky Skaggs to Hitler, that's a scary thought, you know?"

Carter thought about the fine line he had crossed when he broke the Bottleneck Savings and Loan's window, crept inside, and stole what figured to be in the neighborhood of two hundred thousand dollars from his fellow citizens.

The phone rang. Carter took a long swig of coffee and walked over, answering it on the fourth ring. "Hello?"

"Carter? This is the chief. I need you to come down to the station."

"What's up?"

"Tell you when you get here."

$$\sim$$

When Carter arrived at the station, Skeeter was kneeling in front of his filing cabinet, digging frantically through the bottom drawer. A tall, dark-haired man in a gray suit stood behind him, monitoring his progress.

Neither of them looked up as Carter walked hurriedly past and entered Dykes's office without knocking. He found the chief down on all fours, his nose almost pressed to a large, discolored patch of carpeting in front of his desk.

Carter froze, fearing that the old man had suffered a heart attack.

"You all right, Chief?"

"Hell no I'm not all right. I dropped a contac lens right in the middle of this damn coffee stain. Get down here and help me find it."

Carter walked over and knelt beside Dykes. "I didn't know you wore contacs."

"There's a lot you don't know, Carter. For instance, did you know that Rickster's bank got robbed last night?"

"No."

"Well, it sure as hell did. Half the rendering plant's payroll got taken."

"Money for the workers?"

"Yeah. The payroll was insured, so they'll still get paid, but Rickster's worried they'll stop doing business with him if they don't think his bank's safe. Least that's what he said when he called over here pissing and moaning about the whole thing this morning."

"Who's that guy out there with Skeeter?"

"Name's Desmond Kyle. He's FBI," Dykes said, locating his contac and picking it up. He rubbed it between his fingers, tilted his head back, and placed it gently on his retina. A flood of tears immediately welled from his eye and flowed down his cheek.

"FBI?"

"Yeah, that's the best part," Dykes said, walking around his desk and sitting down heavily. "This fed and a bunch of his buddies were laying around up in Austin trying to catch some freak who's been threatening the governor."

"So what's he doing down here?"

"Remember that girl of Rickster's that used to work for him over at the bank? After she left, she got a job as a receptionist at the capital. When Rickster called her and told her what happened, she wigged out. Kyle was right there in the room with her."

"And he just volunteered to investigate a robbery for her?"

"Said he was bored up there, needed a little action. He's already taken a bunch of prints off the bank vault and printed everybody working over there to eliminate them."

"What's he got Skeeter doing out there?"

"Going through our files for any suspicious characters. He wants to check out anybody in the area with any kind of record. Says if nothing else, it'll give us something to do until the print results come back from Austin."

"So he's running the show."

"Looks that way. To tell you the truth, I don't mind having the help. And he seems like a nice enough fella. I don't think you'll have any trouble getting along with him."

"Why would I need to?"

"I'm gonna pair you up with him. I want you to drive him around, help him with his investigation, and just generally keep him the hell out of my hair. Can you do that?"

"What about what Doc Fritch said the other day? I'm supposed to be doing office work, remember? I'm not fit for active duty."

"I don't care a rat's fat ass for what Fritch said. He ain't nothing but a shade-tree psychiatrist anyhow."

Desmond strode into the office, followed closely by Skeeter, who was clutching a manila file folder.

"We found one, Chief," Skeeter said. "Name's Doty Kindel."

"Sounds familiar."

"He's a local boy. Moved back into town a couple of months ago, after he got released from the state pen. He was in for sticking up a feed store in Braintree a few years back. He used a cap gun and made off with twenty bucks."

Skeeter held the folder open for Dykes. Carter craned his neck for a look. Paper-clipped to the upper right-hand corner of the rap sheet inside was the mugshot of an overweight man in his mid-thirties.

Dykes shrugged and Skeeter closed the file, placing it under his arm.

"Might be a good idea to keep an eye on him," Desmond said, "at least until the prints come back. Your man here says his place will be easy for us to look in on."

"Yeah," Skeeter said. "It's within sight of the hunting club me and my brothers belong to. There's a clubhouse up there we can use. Plenty of deer meat in the freezer, too."

"Fine," Dykes said. "Sounds like a complete waste of time to me, but what the hell do I know? Maybe we'll wrap this thing up quick."

"I'd like to go on out there, take a look around," Desmond said.

"Uh, yeah. Desmond Kyle, meet Carter Jackson. He's gonna be your partner for as long as you're here. If that's all right with you, that is."

"Sure," Desmond said, extending his hand. "I'll need all the help I can get finding my way around this place."

Carter shook Desmond's hand. "Just what I always wanted to be. A tour guide."

TWELVE

BETTER THINGS TO DO

Doty Kindel's pea green Barcolounger was in full recline. Sitting in the chair, Doty had to hold the hairy tops of his bare feet as far apart as possible to get an unobstructed view of the new big-screen television set that dominated the small living room. He was flipping back and forth between a minor-league hockey game and an episode of *The Andy Griffith Show* he had seen half a dozen times.

Cecil Keating walked in from the kitchen just as the hockey game went to commercial. He was carrying a plate heaped with hot tamales in one hand and a rumpled magazine in the other. Two cans of beer were cradled in his arm. He dropped one of them onto Doty's ample stomach as he walked past the recliner on his way to the sofa. The beer landed between two plastic freezer bags half-filled with cocaine, which were also resting on Doty's built-in TV tray.

"Who's ahead?" Cecil asked as he sat down on the sofa and began clearing a space on the coffee table for his tamale plate.

He had to push aside three more bags of cocaine, several plastic spoons, and a small scale Doty had used to measure fat grams while on one of his many failed diets. The scale had come in handy of late.

"Houston just scored," Doty said. He picked up the beer, which had begun sliding toward his sinkhole of a bellybutton, and popped the top. He took a long swig from the can, then placed it on the floor beside his chair. Glancing over at Cecil, who was busy stuffing his face and flipping through the magazine, Doty opened one of the bags on his stomach. He stuck a finger inside and deftly scooped a nostrilful of powder up with an overgrown fingernail. He put the finger to his nose, sniffing lightly.

Hearing the faint wheezing, Cecil looked up from his meal.

"I hope to Jesus you're just picking your nose, Doty," he said. "You know we can't afford to be snorting any more of that shit ourselves."

Doty inhaled deeply, then closed the bag, placing it and its brother on the coffee table next to the others. He picked up the remote and switched over to *The Andy Griffith Show*.

"This is a good one," Cecil said, staring up at the screen intently.

Doty nodded in agreement. "Y'know, I saw on CNN the other day where some school way up north—in Michigan I think—was using this show to teach kids about family values."

"Since when do you watch CNN?"

"I watch it all the time," Doty blurted indignantly.

"That's a good idea."

"Yeah, I think it's important to know what's going on in the world. I try to keep up with current events the best I can."

"No, I mean it's a good idea to use this show to teach people how to live. Ought to make the world a better place."

"Oh," Doty sighed. "Well, somebody didn't think it was so smart. They pulled the plug on the whole thing on account of there were hardly ever any niggers in Mayberry."

"You're shitting me!"

"Nope. People said it didn't show what life in America was really like. One big stew pot and all that shit, y'know."

Cecil chased a tamale across the plate with his fork, cut it in two, and guided the more solid half into his mouth. He chewed thoughtfully. "Know what I don't get about that?"

"What?"

"Why don't they just make somebody on the show black? They could colorize them the way that rich guy does with all those old movies."

"Trump?"

"No, that guy who owns all the TV stations. He colorized that movie we watched the other night. The one with Humphrey Bogart in it."

"*Play it Again Sam*," Doty said. "That really was a great movie." He picked up the beer from beside his chair and took a sip as he stared up at the TV. His brow wrinkled.

"Whatcha thinking?" Cecil asked.

"They could make Otis black," Doty said, his eyes sparkling as if he'd just won the lotto. "That would work."

"No it wouldn't," Cecil said chidingly. "The liberals would shit if you made the only nigger in Mayberry the town drunk, too. It would have to be somebody halfway respectable."

"Like Barney?"

"Barney wouldn't make a very convincing soul brother. Besides, he's too important to fool around with. So's Andy."

"What about that Howard guy?"

"The one who always wore a bow tie?"

"Yeah, him."

"You've got the same problem with him that you do with Otis."

"How the hell do you figure that?"

"He was queer, man," Cecil said, exasperated. "Everybody knew it."

"You're nuts," Doty said, turning his beer can up and draining it.

"Think about it, hammerhead. The guy had to be at least forty years old, and he still lived with his mother."

Doty belched. "Maybe you're right."

"You know I am," Cecil said. He popped the last of the tamales into his mouth and washed it down with his beer.

"That leaves Floyd and Goober," Doty said, "and I guess it would have to be Floyd since he owned his own business. Goober was just a flunky."

"Now you're thinking."

Mort, Doty's fat, one-eyed Doberman pinscher, waddled into the room and farted loudly. He made his way to the back door, where he stood looking expectantly over his shoulder at Doty.

"I think that diseased fucking mutt of yours wants out," Cecil said.

Doty got up and let Mort out. He was halfway back to his chair when a long, low bark came from the other side of the door.

"Sounds like he wants back in," Cecil said.

"He's shit out of luck," Doty said, leaning back in the recliner. "I've got better things to do than wait on that dog hand and foot."

Doty flipped back over to the hockey game, where the team from Houston was still leading.

THIRTEEN

MEMBERS ONLY

"W hat the hell's that dog barking at?" Carter grumbled. He was leaning against the hood of his car, tossing pebbles into a small puddle. Each pebble gave rise to a tiny subaquatic mushroom cloud as it struck the loose silt of the puddle's bottom.

Desmond raised his binoculars and focused in on Kindel's house. Three hundred yards of red sand and scrub brush separated the dilapidated shack from the elevated ridge he and Carter were standing on.

"Beats me," he said as he watched the most hideous dog he had ever seen stagger from one end of Kindel's porch to the other, craning its neck and quivering as it brayed like a jackass. "Must be a rabbit or something down there."

Desmond lowered the binoculars and turned to Carter, who was gathering more pebbles from the ground. He tossed one into the puddle, then took careful aim and pitched one at a squirrel scurrying across the roof of the decaying old house the members of Skeeter's hunting club used as a headquarters during deer season.

The pebble missed the squirrel, landing several feet away from it with a barely audible thump. The squirrel dropped the acorn it had been nibbling on and bounded over to the stony projectile, sniffing it and wiggling its tail.

After leaving the highway, Carter and Desmond had negotiated over a mile of twisted logging roads posted with No Trespassing signs to reach the clearing where the house stood. The ridge it was perched upon overlooked several small farms and homesteads, among them Kindel's place. Desmond had been pleased with the house. As soon as Skeeter arrived with the keys, it would make an excellent command post.

Carter threw another pebble at the squirrel, missing again. He tossed the remainder of his ammunition into a clump of weeds and walked around the car to where Desmond stood wiping the lenses of his binoculars with the tip of his tie. "Why don't we just go down there and see if he's got an alibi?"

"Everybody's got an alibi," Desmond said.

"Yeah, but he might have one that checks out. Just because the guy did a little time doesn't mean he hasn't straightened up."

Desmond sighed. "You're really not into this, are you?"

"What's to get into? Whoever took that money was probably just passing through town. They're long gone by now."

"Maybe, but this is the closest thing to a lead we've got right now. We'll watch Kindel for a little while and see if he does anything suspicious."

"Like what?"

"I don't know. Maybe he'll buy a new Cadillac or something."

Desmond looked through his binoculars again. The back of what looked like a late-model Ford Mustang parked on the far side of Kindel's house was partially visible through an uneven hedge growing in the yard. Desmond had walked all along the ridge trying to get a better view of the car, but he had been unable to make out more than the last two digits of the license plate.

"I wish we knew who was driving that Mustang," he said. The only vehicle registered to Kindel was an old pickup, which was resting on cinderblocks in the middle of an overgrown garden off to the side of the house.

"That's probably the getaway car," Carter said sarcastically. "I imagine Kindel and his gang are splitting up the loot right now. We should go down there and bust their asses."

"I don't guess your attitude would have anything to do with your vacation being cut short, would it?" Desmond asked.

"Vacation?"

"The chief told me he had to pull you in from your time off for this. I'd be pissed, too."

Carter shook his head slowly. "I'm not pissed," he said. "I just don't want us to jump to any conclusions."

"You really think somebody from out of town robbed the bank?"

"It sure as hell wouldn't be the first time somebody passing through this town stopped in just to make trouble."

"That a fact?"

"Yeah," Carter said, looking down at his feet. He could feel Desmond staring at him as the sounds of an approaching car became audible. "That must be Skeeter," he said.

Skeeter's car crept slowly around a bend in the bumpy road and rolled to a stop at the edge of the clearing. He and Goolsby got out and meandered over to Carter and Desmond.

"Anything happening?" Skeeter asked.

"Nothing," Desmond said. "Did you bring those keys?"

Skeeter took a pair of freshly cut keys from his pocket and handed one to Desmond. He waved the other in front of Carter's face. "What's the matter? Not enough excitement for you?"

Carter snatched the key and pocketed it as he walked to his car. "Let's get out of here," he said to Desmond. "This place is starting to look like a used car lot."

Desmond turned to Skeeter and Goolsby. "Got any binoculars?"

"In the car," Goolsby said.

"There's a Mustang on the other side of Kindel's house," Desmond said. "Keep an eye on it; see if you can make out the plate if anybody leaves in it."

"No problem," Skeeter said as Desmond walked over to the car and got in. Carter started the engine and guided the car down the road.

"What's eating Carter?" Goolsby asked when they were out of sight.

"Would you want to be stuck up here all morning with that tightass?"

"Guess not."

"C'mon," Skeeter said, walking toward the house and waving for Goolsby to follow him. "Let's go rustle us up something to eat."

FOURTEEN

WHILE THE GETTING'S GOOD

Dakota sat in the booking area of the police station, idly flipping through a tattered hunting magazine she had picked up from the messy coffee table.

She looked up from the magazine at Horace, who was staring at a collage of yellowing wanted posters tacked to the wall. Every few seconds, he would pull his gaze from the posters long enough to make sure Chief Dykes, who was minding the front desk, wasn't surveilling him.

Dakota waited for Horace to look her way. When he did, she made a grand display of rolling her eyes at him and looking disgusted.

"Y'all want a drink?" Dykes asked.

"No thanks," Dakota said.

"We got a soda machine in back. How 'bout a co-cola?"

"Thanks, but I'm not really thirsty. What about you, Horace?"

Horace's head snapped up. "What? Y'all talking to me?"

"You thirsty?"

"Uh, yeah, I could drink a Coke." Horace reached into his pocket for change.

"No charge for Carter's friends," Dykes said. "Be right back." He got up from the desk and disappeared down the hall.

Horace walked over to Dakota, snatching the magazine from her and tossing it onto the coffee table. "What the hell are we doing here, girl?"

"Calm down."

"You're not nervous?"

"Nope."

"Well, I'm getting the hell out of here while the getting's good. See ya."

"See ya."

Horace turned to leave and ran into Carter and Desmond, who were just walking into the station. He lowered his head, sidestepped them, and made his exit without looking up.

Carter noticed Dakota, who had gotten up from the bench.

"Hey," he said. "I'm surprised to see you."

"I just came by to check up on you. How are you feeling?"

"I'm all right," he said. "My head's still a little sore, but I'll live. What was your friend in such a hurry for?"

"He remembered some things that need doing out at the strip."

Desmond cleared his throat.

"Dakota Winslow," Carter said, "this is my new partner, Desmond Kyle."

"Nice to meet you," Desmond said.

"You, too."

"Well," Desmond said, "I'll catch you later, Carter." He walked down the hall and met Dykes, who was carrying Horace's soft drink.

"That for me? Thanks." Desmond snatched the drink from the chief and took a long swig as he walked down the hall. Dykes glowered after him.

Dakota picked up her purse from the bench and shouldered it. "Are you still working?"

"I'm off," Carter said.

"Good," she said. "I'm hungry. You ever eat at Ma's?"

FIFTEEN

PURSUING VENUS

Carter and Dakota sat at a table next to the jukebox in
Ma's Pantry, a greasy spoon on the outskirts of Bottleneck with only two items on its menu: fried chicken and
fried catfish. A plump waitress with her red hair tied back in
a pony tail had just taken their orders.

"Be right back with your drinks," the girl said, putting her
pencil behind her ear and dropping her notepad into one of
the pockets of her blue and white striped apron. She turned
toward the kitchen and nearly ran over a tall, thin wisp of a
woman with a crumpled cigarette dangling from between her
lips.

"'Scuse me, honey," the woman slurred. She walked over
to the jukebox and dropped two quarters into the slot, punching in her selections with a shaking finger.

"Who's the kid in the picture on your desk?" Carter asked.

"That's my son," Dakota said. She had been fidgeting with
her napkin since they sat down. She now unfolded it and
placed it on her lap. "His name's Brian."

"What's with that outfit?"

"He goes to a military academy in San Antonio. It takes everything I make to keep him there, but it's worth it. The schools around here aren't good for much except turning out more farmers."

Carter took a cigarette from his shirt pocket and lit it, realizing too late that there wasn't an ashtray on the table.

"Does his father help out," he asked, exhaling.

"No."

The wisp woman turned and shuffled slowly toward the other side of the room as her first selection, Nanci Griffith's version of Kate Wolf's "Across the Great Divide," began playing.

"This is such a pretty song," Dakota said. "But sad, too. The first time I heard it I was on the way home from my father's funeral. I pulled over to the side of the road and just listened until it was over."

Carter flicked an ash onto the floor. "How'd your father die?"

"He flew his plane into a power line on his way back from a job. The coroner said it looked like he fell asleep, but I don't know how he could tell anything like that. Daddy was burnt up pretty bad."

"I remember hearing about that."

"Yeah, it made all the papers. The TV news, too. It was a big story, I guess."

"So you inherited the business from your father?"

"Yeah."

"And Horace?"

"I guess you could say I inherited him too. He was with Daddy from the beginning, so it would've been a little weird just letting him go."

"You just keep him around out of the kindness of your heart, huh?"

Dakota shook her head. "He's a good enough mechanic. He earns his keep."

The waitress walked over with Carter's beer and Dakota's iced tea. She flashed a sweet smile and was gone.

Carter looked around to see if anyone was watching him, then stubbed his cigarette out on the floor. He tossed the butt into the corner, where a small pile of rubbish sat pushed up against the bristles of an abandoned broom.

"So how'd your father settle on the name Venus for a sky-writing service?" he asked, sipping his beer. "Did he name it after your mama?"

"No, not hardly. She ran out on us when I was just three years old. He named the place for his brother, my Uncle Harvey."

Dakota told Carter the story of her Uncle Harvey, who had been a fighter pilot stationed on an air force base in New Mexico at the height of the cold war. It was common practice in those days to scramble jets every time an unidentified blip appeared on a radar screen. Harvey had faced down airborne threats ranging from flocks of Canadian Geese to private pilots whose planes had strayed off course, but he always returned safely to the base none the worse for wear and with his full compliment of missiles still in place.

All that changed one night in the spring of 1974 during an outbreak of unidentified aerial sightings that plagued air bases across the country. Harvey went up expecting to encounter another flock of geese. Half an hour later, an emergency ground crew was prying his body from the twisted wreckage of his plane, which had plummeted to the desert floor.

The official explanation of his brother's death had never sat well with Dakota's father. It stated that Harvey had passed out due to oxygen deprivation while pursuing the planet Venus, which was "clearly visible to the naked eye on the night in question."

Dakota's father wasn't the only one dissatisfied with the explanation. Several of Harvey's fighter pilot buddies contacted him over the years to offer support. One said that he had seen a classified report on the incident that stated Harvey's plane had been shot down by a craft of unknown origin.

Another, who'd served on the ground crew, told him that all but one of Harvey's missiles had been fired.

Dakota remembered her father writing countless letters to the government requesting more information, then staying up late into the night and pouring over the heavily edited documents they sent him in reply. Fifteen years after Harvey's fatal crash, he had gone to his own fiery death, still firmly convinced that his brother had been killed in a dogfight with a flying saucer.

"He never got over it," she said, moving her tea aside for the waitress, who had just arrived at their table with a pair of freshly washed plates and a basket of catfish. "Pretty strange, huh?"

"I don't know," Carter said. "Not really."

The waitress left them. Carter picked up his beer bottle and tapped it against Dakota's glass. "Here's to your old man," he said. "At least he knew what he believed in."

Dakota studied Carter's face as he took a long pull from his beer and began piling catfish onto his plate.

SIXTEEN

THE UNINVITED GUEST

Dakota stood at her door, watching Carter's taillights fade as he drove back toward town. She fumbled around in her purse for her keys, found them, and entered the trailer. Flipping on the lights, she gasped at the sight of Horace sprawled across her couch.

"What the hell are you doing in here?"

"Just making sure you got home all right," Horace said, sitting up and stretching.

"I'm fine, now get out of here."

"Where you been?"

"Not that it's any of your business, but me and Carter had dinner at Ma's."

"Carter? So you're on a first name basis now."

"That's right."

"What did you have? Chicken or fish?"

"Fish."

"Sounds pretty serious. You like him?"

"He's a nice guy."

Horace jumped up from the couch and lunged at Dakota, grabbing her arm and twisting it behind her back. "Well you're not a nice girl, Dakota. Remember that."

"Let go of me, you slob!" Dakota swung her purse, catching Horace on the side of the head and knocking him to the floor. He scrambled to his feet and ran from the trailer.

Dakota bolted the front door. Grabbing her purse, she ran to the bathroom, where she fell to her knees in front of the toilet and vomited. She leaned her head against the basin and cried for a long time, then got up and walked to the sink.

She took a stab at fixing her disheveled hair but gave up. Opening her purse, she took out a small vial of cocaine and trailed a line on the countertop. Pressing one nostril closed, she bowed her head and snorted it.

SEVENTEEN

THE GOOD WORD

The FBI usually shied away from artsy types. There was only so much creativity needed to tap phone lines and plow through income tax records, so the starched collars running the show from the J. Edgar Hoover Building in Washington, D.C., had little use for dreamers.

Despite this fact, Desmond hadn't had any trouble parlaying his liberal arts degree from New York University into a law enforcement career that had so far been viewed as promising by his superiors. He accomplished this by using a method employed by job seekers in every industry and field of service fortunate enough to know connected people: the good word.

Desmond's good word had been put in for him by his cousin Donald, who didn't even work for the FBI. Donald was, in fact, a criminal, a mafia accountant who had turned state's evidence and gone into the witness protection program when federal agents targeted his employer.

Donald was working at the time for Bruno Hopper, the proprietor of several upscale men's clothing stores in New York City. The stores served as a front for a hive of illegal activities ranging from narcotics distribution to loan sharking.

When approached by a pair of agents with the news that his boss was one of the most diversified and successful criminals on the East Coast, Donald hadn't been particularly surprised. He had known almost from day one that the company he worked for wasn't completely legitimate. The huge sums of cash he was constantly being instructed to divert to bank accounts in South America had clued him in.

But he had been disappointed. He made good money at his job, worked with nice—though sometimes shady—people, and found it thrilling. While his fellow bean counters were struggling to guide their clients through greased loopholes, he was dealing with millions of dollars on an almost daily basis.

The thrill began to fade, however, when the government offered him a choice between testifying against his boss or serving a prison sentence. For Donald, the decision was easy. He took the deal and saved his ass.

After his testimony made sure that his employer and most of his co-workers would never breathe clean air again, Donald went into hiding. Every six months or so, his handlers would parade him into a courtroom to testify against some former business associate of Hopper's who had been apprehended. Over the years, he had gotten pretty chummy with the agents charged with his safekeeping, advising them at tax time, sometimes helping them hoodwink the very government signing their paychecks.

Everybody loved it, and everybody at the bureau thought Donald was a swell guy. No one seemed to care that he had once gleefully overseen the financing of a slew of criminal activities, or that once confronted, he had turned and viciously mauled the dirty hand feeding him. And most importantly, no one had ever held his criminal's good word against Desmond.

After checking into Bottleneck's only hotel, the Inn and Out, Desmond tried to call his cousin. The agent who answered the phone informed him that Donald was playing golf and wouldn't be in for at least a couple of hours.

After a few minutes of friendly chitchat, Desmond hung up and pulled a large sketch pad from his suitcase. He made a habit of keeping a sketch diary of each case he worked on and had so far filled over a dozen such pads with drawings of criminals and temporary allies. He flipped open the pad and dashed off a rendering of Chief Dykes, then one of the Inn and Out's clerk. He got bored with her rather bland face and finished her with a stick figure's body and a pair of cartoonishly large breasts.

Finally, he worked his way around to Carter. He took his time, carefully sketching the wiry frame and the wrinkled uniform. When he got to the face, he drew its outline and fixed it with a nose and mouth but left blank spaces where the eyes belonged when he couldn't remember their exact shape.

Ripping the page from the pad, Desmond balled it up and tossed it into a wastebasket beside the night stand, resolving to pay a little more attention to his new partner the next day.

EIGHTEEN

WINDOW DRESSING

D amn your cheating ass!" Del screamed. He jumped to his feet and raked his arm across the card table, sending the chessboard and the pieces still on it flying across the front of the pawn shop.

"That tears it, Del," Jimmy said, standing up and bringing his bony fist down hard on the table.

Carter turned toward the commotion and shook his head as he watched Del lunge for Jimmy's throat, his gnarled fingers poised to throttle him. Jimmy stepped to the side, and Del fell in a heap on the floor.

"I can't believe what I'm seeing," Carter said. "Two grown men who've been friends for thirty years ready to kill each other over a damn game. I should lock you both up. In the same cell."

"You couldn't lock him up with anybody else," Del said, climbing to his feet. "They'd be trading his shriveled ass back and forth for cigarettes."

Del and Jimmy sat back down across the table from each

other, both of them breathing heavily and staring forlornly at their scattered game.

Carter turned back to the counter. He had come in to get his shotgun out of hock and could hear Ben rattling around in the back of the store, where he kept the recently pawned items.

The bell above the door rang as Desmond strode into the shop. He stopped and nodded a good morning to Del and Jimmy, both of whom were still panting from the excitement of their skirmish.

Carter turned and felt the hairs on the back of his neck stiffen when he saw Desmond standing just inside the door, eyeing Del and Jimmy curiously. It was all he could do to force a smile in acknowledgement of his new partner's wave.

"What are you doing here?" Desmond asked, walking over to the counter and leaning on it next to Carter.

"Just picking up a gun of mine," Carter replied, his mouth suddenly dry. "I pawned it for a little spending money before I left on my vacation. What about you?"

Desmond was staring down through the counter's glass top at a pair of throwing knives, on the blades of which a previous owner had painted the words "peace" and "love."

"I've been walking up and down the strip here asking people if they've seen any suspicious activity around the bank," he said. "I know it's a long shot, but maybe somebody saw a stranger hanging around, casing the place."

Desmond looked over his shoulder at Del and Jimmy, who had recovered enough to begin gathering their chess pieces from the floor. "What about you two?" he asked.

"What about what?" Del growled, plunking a handful of chess pieces down on the board. He began setting them up for a new game.

"The bank robbery," Desmond said. "You fellas see anybody around lately who looked out of place?"

"Just you," Jimmy said. He and Del chuckled.

"Why don't you two try and help out," Carter said. "This is Desmond Kyle, with the FBI. You'll probably end up on his list of suspects if you don't cooperate."

"All I got to say is what I told you the other day, Carter," Jimmy said. "Half this town could've broke that window and cracked the safe. The combination's no big secret."

"What's that supposed to mean?" Desmond asked.

"The safe's combination is the same as the banker's daughter's birthday," Del said. "The dumb little snot couldn't remember it any other way."

Ben emerged from the back of the store with Carter's shotgun. Carter took a pair of hundred dollar bills from his pocket.

"What the hell was all that racket?" Ben said, taking the money from Carter's hand and punching a key on the cash register.

"Your window dressing is starting to come unraveled," Carter said. He reached across the counter and accepted his change with one hand and his gun with the other.

"How much for these knives?" Desmond asked.

"Fifteen bucks," Ben said.

"I'll take 'em," Desmond said. He took out his wallet and withdrew a crisp twenty.

"You know how to throw those things?" Carter asked.

"Well enough," Desmond said. He took the knives from Ben and stuffed them into his coat pocket. "You on your way to the station?"

"Yeah."

"I'll walk you over."

NINETEEN

ART APPRECIATION

A re you sure you didn't have a little too much to drink the other night, Stu?" Chief Dykes asked, reclining in his swivel chair and clasping his hands across his stomach. "Liquor'll do odd things to a man's vision. I know you know that."

"Chief," Stu said, his voice trembling, "I was tight as a gnat's ass stretched over a rain barrel, but I know what I saw."

Stu brought his finger down hard on the rough sketch lying on the chief's desk. "That's what I saw. No doubt in my mind about it."

Dykes leaned forward and brushed Stu's hand aside. "Hands off my drawing, boy," he said, picking up the sketch. It was of a lanky man wearing a mask and lugging what looked like an oversized briefcase.

There was a knock at the door. Carter ambled in, followed by Desmond.

"Yeah, come on in," Dykes mumbled. He tossed the sketch into the air, letting it waft back to the desk. He fixed Stu with a disapproving stare.

"What's up?" Carter asked.

"Oh, not much," Dykes said. "Just looks like the crazies are already coming out of the woodwork for that reward."

"What reward?" Desmond asked.

"That idiot Rickster bought time on the radio this morning to let everybody know he was offering fifty thousand bucks for information about the robbery. Not an hour later, Stu here comes wandering in with his tall tale."

"Hell, Chief," Stu said, "I didn't even know about any damn reward until I got here and you told me about it."

Desmond walked over to Dykes's desk and looked at the sketch. "Who drew this?"

"He did," Dykes said, pointing at Stu.

"So Spiderman robbed the bank?" Desmond said, handing the sketch to Carter. "Somehow I don't think so."

A chill ran down Carter's spine. Stu had done a pretty fair job with the likeness. He turned to Stu. "What were you doing downtown at night?"

"My friends wouldn't give me a ride home. It's a long story."

"And I don't think I can sit through it again," Dykes said, looking from Carter to Desmond. "Anyway, it checks out."

Desmond nodded. "We're going out to relieve Skeeter and Goolsby at the club," he said. "We'll keep our eyes open for any masked men."

Desmond walked out. Carter handed the sketch to Stu and followed him.

Stu looked up at the chief, then carefully folded the sketch, which was beginning to smudge, and stuffed it into his shirt pocket.

"Yeah, go ahead," Dykes said. "I wouldn't wipe my ass with that thing."

TWENTY

SHORT SUBJECTS

When Carter and Desmond arrived at the camp, Skeeter and Goolsby's patrol car was nowhere in sight. They went inside and found Goolsby asleep on an old couch in what had once been the house's living room. The walls were adorned with the heads of unfortunate deer and the stuffed carcasses of oversized bass and waterfowl.

Carter walked over to the couch. A tin plate on which the vestiges of a venison and potatoes meal was now growing cold rose and fell on Goolsby's stomach as he snored. Carter nudged him, and he awoke.

"Hey, fellas," Goolsby said, sitting up and sending the plate crashing to the floor. He ran his hand through his hair and stared at the mess. "Damn. What time is it?"

"Almost nine," Desmond said. He walked over and picked up the plate and the bits of food that had fallen from it. He carried the mess over to the garbage can in the corner and tossed it in, plate and all.

"Where's Skeeter?" Carter asked, walking over to the

window.

"He went into town for coffee. He ought to be back directly."

Carter parted the curtains and peered down at Kindel's house. "They're gone."

"Yeah, they took off early this morning in that Mustang. The plate number's over there."

"Where?" Desmond asked.

"There," Goolsby said, pointing at a pile of crumpled napkins on the floor beside a beat-up old chair. "It's written on one of those."

Desmond sifted through the napkins and found the one with the number scrawled on it. He wadded it up again and tossed it to Goolsby. "Run the number as soon as you get back to town, all right?"

"You got it."

The sound of a car could be heard. It stopped just outside the house and one of its doors squeaked open, then slammed shut hard.

"That'll be Skeeter," Goolsby said, getting up from the couch.

Skeeter walked into the trophy room carrying a medium-sized paper sack. He set it down on the floor and it fell over, spilling its contents onto the rug. There were two cans of coffee, several bags of pork rinds, and a collection of snack cakes.

"Thought you said there was plenty of food out here," Carter said.

"There is, if you want to go to the trouble to cook it. Me and Goolsby nearly burned the place down using that old hot plate in the kitchen."

Desmond took the "love" knife from his pocket, gripped it firmly by the blade, and tossed it at the scattered groceries.

It skewered a package of Twinkies.

"What the hell'd you do that for?" Goolsby asked.

Desmond shrugged and walked over to the window. He took his binoculars from their case and studied Kindel's house.

"Guess we'll be heading out," Skeeter said.

"See y'all later," Carter said.

Skeeter and Goolsby walked out. After a few seconds, Carter heard their car start up and pull away. He turned to Desmond.

"What's the matter with you?"

"Why didn't you tell me about the bank safe?" Desmond asked, lowering the binoculars but continuing to stare out the window.

"I guess it slipped my mind."

Desmond walked over to the mess on the floor and retrieved his knife from the Twinkies. He wiped the blade on the arm of the couch, leaving a cream smear. "If what those old guys said is true, anybody in town could have robbed the bank."

Carter nodded.

"I'm going down there," Desmond said.

"Down where?"

"To Kindel's house. I'll go in and look around for anything incriminating."

"I don't think going down there's a good idea."

"I'm out of good ideas. Might as well start trying some of the bad ones."

∾

Desmond stepped onto the back porch and froze. Kindel's dog, which was roughly the size of a Shetland pony, lay sleeping beside an old milk can at the far end of the porch.

Keeping one eye on the dog, Desmond crept up to the back door and tried it. It was locked. He took his wallet out and removed a credit card from it. The card slid easily between the door and the frame, and he was able to trip the latch in just a few seconds. He replaced the card and put his wallet away, turning toward the ridge and waving his arms. He knew Carter would be watching through the binoculars.

Inside the house, Desmond was almost floored by an odor that was a cross between stale beer and an armpit. He was standing in a cramped room into which was packed a recliner, a sofa and a big-screen television. The TV looked new. He walked around, scanning the room. There was a residue of white powder on the dirty coffee table in front of the sofa.

Desmond ran a finger through the powder and brought it to his lips. Thinking of the room's aroma and general squalor, he couldn't bring himself to touch his tongue to it. He wiped his finger on his jacket. Probably just powdered sugar from a donut, he thought. Kindel certainly looked like he'd been throwing back his share of junk food.

There was a small kitchen adjoining the den. On the counter was a half-empty jar of salsa around which were scattered several crumbling corn chips. Desmond went through the cabinets and drawers but found no stolen loot.

Kindel's bedroom was surprisingly neat. The bed was made, and there were no wrinkles in the covers. Desmond searched the chest of drawers and had a look inside the small closet. Finding nothing, he was about to leave the room when he spotted something sticking out from under the bed.

He walked over and got down on one knee for a closer look.

The object protruding from under the bed was a metal strongbox. Taking it by the corner, Desmond pulled the box across the thick carpeting into the center of the bedroom. There was no padlock, and the lid swung open easily.

Inside were five plastic bags filled with white powder and a videocassette. He opened one of the bags and this time mustered the courage to taste the substance. It was cocaine. He closed the bag, placed it back in the box, and removed the tape.

Back in the den, he found an ancient VCR beside the television. He popped the tape in and sat down on the couch to watch. The scenes that flashed before his eyes were of a party that had taken place at the house.

Kindel and another man were sitting on the sofa. The sound was bad, but he could make out Kindel calling his friend "Cecil." Also, there was a slender, auburn-haired woman. She was kneeling at the coffee table, her back to the camera's eye. Something about her struck Desmond as familiar.

The woman threw her head back and turned to face the camera, wiping coke from her upper lip with the back of her hand. It was the girl who had been waiting at the police station for Carter the day before. Dakota something or other.

Desmond felt like he had been kicked in the stomach. She turned back to the table and lowered her head for one last snort before standing up and walking toward the camera. The picture bounced about as the camera changed hands, Dakota now doing the filming. Her friend, the one in the jumpsuit, had apparently been holding the camera before. He loped into the frame and ran his finger through the cocaine on the table, then smeared it across his front teeth.

Desmond got up and stopped the tape, pulling it from the machine. He walked over to the window and looked toward the clubhouse on the ridge in the distance. Turning, he walked into the bedroom and placed the tape back into the strongbox, which he closed and slid back under the bed.

TWENTY-ONE

SMOOTH AS SNAKES

"You ever wonder what it would be like if you could go back in time?"

"What the hell are you talking about?"

"Going back in time, like in a time machine. People were more simple-minded back then. You'd be like a genius."

Cecil was leaning across the hood of his Mustang, examining the windshield. He and Doty had gotten caught behind a gravel truck on their way out to the airstrip, and there were several small chips in the glass from the tiny rocks that showered the car each time the truck hit a dip in the road.

He stood up straight and looked at Doty, who was seated on the trunk of the car, desperately trying to open a can of beer. Cecil had talked him into clipping his fingernails that morning.

"What the hell's the matter with you?" Cecil asked, walking around to the rear of the car. "Are you junked up?"

"No," Doty said as he continued to try and force the tip of his index finger under the can's tab. "Why?"

"What's with this time travel shit? And when the hell do you think people were any more 'simple-minded' than your stupid ass is right here today?"

"I just meant that you'd have a real head start on things. You could invent the light bulb before Einstein ever even got the idea."

Cecil snatched the beer can away from Doty. He shook it hard, pointed the business end at his partner, and popped the top. Doty tried to shield himself with his arms as a thick stream of suds shot from the can to soak his face.

"Asshole!" he yelled. "You can damage somebody's vision like that!"

Cecil grabbed Doty's hand and shoved the now half-empty can into it. "You know what I'd do if I could go back in time? I'd go back to the day you were conceived and shoot your daddy before he got a chance to knock your poor mama up. I'd save myself a whole hell of a lot of trouble."

"No need to get personal."

"Your shortcut's gonna cost me a new windshield, Doty. I don't mind you knowing I'm pissed off."

"I can't believe you're worried about money," Doty said. He took a long swig from the can and wiped his mouth with his shirt sleeve. "Once we get this thing good and set up, you'll be able to buy all the glass you want."

Cecil cocked his head. "You hear that?" he asked, cupping his hand to his ear.

"Yeah, it's the plane," Doty said, crushing the beer can and tossing it to the ground. He hopped down from the car and stood beside Cecil.

The two of them watched as the plane appeared. It was

flying over the tree line that bordered the far end of the clearing into which the runway was cut.

The plane banked and flew toward the runway. It dipped as if to come in for a landing, then rose sharply, its engine whining.

"What the hell's she doing?" Doty asked.

"Beats me," Cecil said, watching Doty from the corner of his eye. "She's probably stoned, just like you."

Doty sighed and shifted his considerable weight. Cecil turned his gaze back to the plane. He and Doty continued to watch as it flew directly over their heads, releasing a cloud of smoke as it passed.

"Shit," Cecil said as the cloud fell around them. He and Doty ran for the shelter of the hangar, coughing and rubbing at their eyes.

Inside, Cecil blinked his eyes rapidly until his vision cleared. He saw Horace sitting behind the desk at the far end of the hangar, punching the keys of an adding machine. He stopped and looked up at them, the corner of his mouth curling into a grin.

"What the hell's her problem?" Doty howled. "She tried to gas us!"

"Relax," Horace said, getting up and walking around the desk. "That shit's fairly harmless."

"Fairly?" Cecil asked. He walked over and sat down on the sofa next to the desk.

"Well, you probably won't have to worry about any excess body hair," Horace said. "You'll both be smooth as snakes by morning."

"You mean that shit makes your hair fall out?" Doty asked, running his fingers through his greasy black shock.

"He's just fucking with you," Cecil said. He turned to

Horace and eyed him seriously. "You are just screwing around, right?"

"Yeah. At the most you might develop a mild rash, kinda like diaper rash, but all over your body. It ain't so bad."

Cecil leaned back on the couch and crossed his legs. "When can you make another pick up?"

"How's distribution going?"

"All right. Me and Doty have been getting the word out, y'know, making some contacts. We're building up a good consumer base."

"Well, I can go down anytime. Just set it up with your guy and give me the word."

"What about Dakota?"

"She'll keep going along with it. She's got no choice, really."

"Good. I think we'll get out of here before she decides to make another pass," Cecil said, standing up. "You're, uh, sure about the hair, right?"

"Positive," Horace said, catching Doty's uneasy gaze and winking. "Smooth as snakes."

TWENTY-TWO

CAN'T GET THERE FROM HERE

Carter guided the cruiser slowly along the logging trail, careful not to let the wheels fall into line with the deep, rain-filled grooves worn into the road by countless pulpwood trucks and hunter laden four-wheel drives. He lit a cigarette and rolled down the window.

Desmond sat in the passenger seat, staring glassily out the window. He squinted as he watched swarms of fat tadpoles, still reveling in the blissful throes of amphibian adolescence, dart to and fro in the flooded ruts.

"Hey," Desmond said, still staring at the trail, "what say we stop somewhere on the way back to town and grab a beer?"

Carter began braking as the car bounced toward the end of the logging trail, which terminated in a quagmire of gravel and sludge before it joined the pristine surface of the highway.

"I need to get on back to town," he said.

"Got a hot date?"

Carter chuckled. "I don't know how hot it'll be," he said. "Have I got it that way?"

Desmond checked for oncoming cars. "It's clear."

The car lurched onto the highway. Carter rolled his window up until only about a half inch of open air remained. He took a drag from his cigarette and eased the burning stem out the window, trailing a shower of sparks.

"Who are you taking out?" Desmond asked, clearing his throat and trying his best to sound nonchalant. "That girl from the station?"

"Yeah. We're not going out, actually, just having dinner at her place."

"She seems like a nice girl."

"Seems like it." Carter rolled the window down a few more inches and tossed the remainder of his cigarette out. He watched in the rearview mirror as the smoldering butt bounced and broke up on the highway.

"You'll have to get Skeeter or Goolsby to be-bop around with you tomorrow," he said.

"Why's that?"

"I'm taking the day off to take care of some personal business out of town."

Desmond nodded. The two of them remained silent for the next several miles of highway. Finally, as Carter slowed to avoid rear-ending an ancient Buick creeping glacially along the road, Desmond spoke.

"You're about my age, right?"

"I'm twenty-six," Carter said, passing the Buick and tapping his horn twice as he did so. The elderly black man driving the huge car gave him the tall man.

"I'm twenty-eight," Desmond said. "Did you ever watch wrestling when you were a kid?"

"Sure, all the time."

"Remember the Masked Marvel?"

"Yeah. I never liked him much, though."

"Me neither, but he wore a mask like the one that guy at the station described."

"Oh yeah, you're right. Maybe we should find out where this Masked Marvel's been keeping himself, focus our search on a fat guy in tights."

"I don't know where we should focus anything, smartass. I was just thinking out loud."

Carter's dash-mounted radio crackled to life. "Carter?" Chief Dykes's voice boomed from the tiny speaker. "Carter, you there?"

Carter picked up the receiver. "Yeah, Chief, this is me."

"I don't suppose you've got your new best friend there with you?"

Carter rolled his eyes and passed the receiver to Desmond, who accepted it with a grin. "This is Agent Kyle, Chief. Go ahead."

"We got the results back on those fingerprints you took off the safe. All the sets but one match up with somebody working there at the bank."

"And?"

"Well, those extra prints ain't Kindel's. There wasn't any match for them."

"Thanks for calling," Desmond said, putting the receiver back in its place. He looked over at Carter, expecting a smart remark, but there was none. Carter simply drove, his eyes glued to the road ahead.

≈

Carter eased the car into the parking lot of the Inn and Out and stopped in front of the manager's office. Desmond stepped out.

"Good luck," he said, slamming the door.

Carter waved as he pulled away. Desmond watched the car disappear around the corner and fumbled for his keys as he walked to his room. Inside, he kicked his shoes off and collapsed on the bed, taking the remote from the night stand and flipping quickly through the dozens of free cable channels offered by the hotel. He paused for a moment on an adult feature, but his heart wasn't in it.

He finally settled on a movie channel. One of his all-time favorites, William Peter Blatty's *The Ninth Configuration*, was playing. It was about halfway through the movie, which centered around a special forces colonel who goes insane after beheading a young Vietnamese boy with a wire while slaughtering Cong soldiers behind enemy lines.

The colonel, known throughout the corps as Killer Kane, adopts the identity of his brother, a psychiatrist at an institution specializing in the treatment of mentally disturbed servicemen. By helping the patients there, Kane hopes to wash the blood from his hands.

Desmond watched as Kane, played by Stacy Keach, listened intently to the fears of fallen astronaut Billy Cutshaw, played by Scott Wilson. Cutshaw had been institutionalized after bolting from his space capsule seconds before being blasted toward the moon. He had been driven over the edge by the fear that if he died on the moon, he wouldn't be able to find his way to Heaven.

Desmond watched the film for half an hour or so, then drifted off and dreamed fitfully about the videotape of Kindel's party. In his dream, he walked around the filthy room, an invisible observer to the sordid goings on.

He was awakened by the sound of two cats who were screaming at each other somewhere on the Inn and Out's grounds. He got up, undressed down to his underwear, and walked to the window. He pulled aside the thickly woven curtains and peered out at the deserted parking lot and the bleak Bottleneck landscape, wondering whether or not he would make it to Heaven if anything happened to him this far from home.

TWENTY-THREE

WHERE THERE'S SMOKE

After dropping Desmond off at the hotel, Carter began to get a bit nervous about his impending dinner date with Dakota. Swapping stories over catfish at Ma's Pantry was one thing, but actually driving out to the home of this girl he only knew because she had nearly killed him was another.

During the course of going home, showering, and getting dressed, however, the butterflies in his stomach were replaced by a gnawing hunger—the result of having Twinkies for lunch. As he drove out to Dakota's, he thought more about what she might be serving for dinner than anything else.

Dakota's double-wide trailer was situated near the highway on a rectangular lot just a few hundred yards from the airstrip. Carter stepped up onto Dakota's porch. The door was slightly ajar, and thin wisps of black smoke were wafting from inside. He knocked and pushed the door open.

"Should I call the fire department?" he asked, stepping into the small living room. He could see Dakota standing over the stove in the kitchenette, struggling over a steak so large it hung over the edges of the pan she was using. She maneuvered the slab deftly about with a huge two-pronged fork.

"I don't think it's that bad yet," she said. "I had to take the batteries out of the smoke detector, though. It kept going off."

Carter walked into the kitchen. "Need any help?"

"I'll manage. Why don't you have a seat in there and I'll call you when everything's ready. I got started a little late."

Carter walked back into the den. He sat down on the sofa and picked up a photo album from the end table. Most of the pictures were of Dakota's son. A picture of an older man standing next to a small plane on the airstrip must've been of her father, he thought.

The last picture in the album was of Dakota's wedding, but the half of the photo that had once borne the image of her groom had been carefully cut away. The only evidence that the photo was of anything more than Dakota modeling her wedding gown for friends and family was a large, sunburned hand and part of a tuxedo-sleeved forearm resting on her hip.

Carter felt a tap on his shoulder. He snapped the album shut and cleared his throat to hide the sound of his growling stomach.

"Nice dress, huh?" Dakota said, taking the album from his hands.

"Yeah."

"Steaks are ready."

As they ate, Dakota made most of the small talk while Carter devoured his steak and worked on the mountain of green peas she had heaped onto his plate. When they had finished, she took their plates to the sink and began washing leftover peas down the garbage disposal.

"The steak was great," Carter said, getting up from the table and walking over to the couch.

"Thanks," she said, yelling a little over the hum of the disposal. "The peas were a little mushy, though. I think I cooked them too long."

"They were fine. You just cooked too many."

"What?"

"Nothing."

After a few minutes, Dakota turned off the disposal and joined Carter on the sofa. She sat beside him, leaning into him slightly.

"Where is he?" Carter asked.

"Who?"

"The guy you cut out of the wedding picture."

She shifted away from him and brushed a stray lock of hair from her forehead with the back of her hand.

"Sorry," Carter said. "I don't guess it's any of my business."

"That's all right. His name's Curt Samms, and I married him because I was pregnant with Brian. I knew before we got married that he slept around, but he had a good job, and I couldn't stand humiliating my father by being unwed and pregnant. I'd have been the talk of the county, and I couldn't do that to him.

"Not long after that, my father was killed. I had a business to run, and I sure as hell didn't need the bother of staying married to the biggest male slut around. There wasn't anybody left to worry about keeping up appearances for except Brian, and Curt never spent much time with him anyway."

"What happened to him?"

"He got fired from his job right after we split up. Got caught running around with his supervisor's wife, I think.

Last I heard, he was selling insurance somewhere in Oklahoma. So what's your story? Ever been married?"

"Nope."

"Why not? Just haven't found the right girl yet?"

Carter hesitated. "I think I need to have a better idea about where I'm going before I try and take somebody along with me, y'know?"

"Maybe you just need somebody to help you think up a plan."

"Maybe."

Dakota leaned forward, and Carter met her. As they kissed, he reached around her and switched off the lamp on the end table.

TWENTY-FOUR

PIE FACE ERIKSON'S LIVING HELL

Pie Face Erikson's real name was Kendrick, but everyone—
childhood friends, sweethearts, even members of his own
family—had always called him Pie Face. To anyone meeting
him for the first time, the monicker's source was evident.
Erikson's broad, bland countenance resembled nothing so
much as a freshly baked pie with a set of childlike, almost
cherubic features lovingly chiseled into the center.

Upon his graduation from high school, Kendrick's parents
had presented him with a handsome, leather bound ledger
with the inscription "To 'Pie Face' From Mom and Dad"
pressed into the cover. He took the ledger with him to
Louisiana State University, where he majored in business.
Pie Face had a head for it and was at the top of all his
classes.

While at LSU, he roomed with Eric Salazar, an exchange
student from Mexico City. The two soon became fast friends,
partly because they shared common interests such as fishing
and soft-core pornography, and partly because Eric always

seemed to have scads of cash at his disposal, which he was more than willing to spend on or loan out to pals.

After a few months, Eric let Pie Face in on the source of his never-ending stream of revenue. He was the biggest drug supplier on campus, dealing dope of all sorts to the more open-minded members of the student population. Eric would bring the drugs, easily obtained in Mexico, home with him from spring, summer, and holiday vacations, and he had no trouble unloading them as quickly as he made them available.

Pie Face was soon a partner, and his and Eric's little enterprise boomed once he applied his business wizardry to his roommate's hitherto haphazard system of distribution.

Halfway through his sophomore year, Pie Face's parents were killed in a train wreck. Both had taken out life insurance policies years earlier, policies in which their son was named as the sole beneficiary. After a week of introspection following their funerals, Pie Face decided, after conferring with his partner in crime, that they would drop out of school and take their business to a new level.

With Pie Face's innate business sense, Eric's inexaustable connections, and enough cash to effectively finance both, the venture soared. The premise upon which Pie Face had decided to found it was novel. He and Eric would steer clear of distributing their drugs in urban centers, thereby avoiding highly organized law enforcement agencies and the inevitable turf wars with entrenched dealers.

They would instead franchise out their operations, concentrating their distribution efforts in rural areas previously unoccupied and underserved by dealers, areas where the police were more or less harmless.

The system worked well, the only problems arising from

the few instances when Pie Face had allowed Eric to make administrative decisions regarding prospective franchisees. These decisions invariably led to business being conducted in a sloppy manner and to the eventual elimination of the trouble-making partners.

Eric was currently not around to help in cleaning up the messes he had created because of a conviction for having sex with a minor. It was just as well. Pie Face, in the month since Eric's incarceration, had managed to clear up all but one of the problems.

Now, waking up from an hour-long beach nap in front of his beautiful, northern Mexico, ocean-front home, Pie Face's thoughts were not on that lingering problem, which involved a couple of hicks in Texas, but rather on the hideous sunburn covering half his face. He touched his left cheek, winced, and began trudging toward the house.

Opening the sliding glass door, Pie Face stepped inside and kicked Buff, his Siamese cat, across the expansive living room. Buff caromed off the wall, fell to the ground, and licked his genitals. Four years as Pie Face's only round-the-clock companion had conditioned the animal to such treatment.

Pie Face turned and looked at his reflection in the glass door. His face looked like a junkie pieman's entry into a baking contest. Fuming, he walked over to his desk and hit the button on his answering machine for his messages. There was only one.

"Hey, uh, Mr. Pie Face," Cecil Keating's voice seeped from the machine's speaker, "me and Doty's spread around most of the stuff. We were wondering when we could send our guy down for another load. You can call us back any time, okay?"

Pie Face brought his fist down on the answering machine and threw it at Buff, who sidestepped it, fell to the ground, and began purring. Pie Face eyed him disgustedly. Spread around, my ass, he thought. He hadn't seen one red cent from that location. Those two idiots were probably snorting half the shit and passing the rest out to their redneck, pickup-truck-driving buddies.

He picked up the phone and dialed a number he had committed to memory when these problems first began cropping up.

Over a hundred miles away, in the small town of Benton, Louisiana, the phone in the office of the Ascending Spirit Church rang.

Reverend Edgar Otto, known to the thirty or so members of his flock as Reverend Ed and to Pie Face and a very few others as the Crucifixer, was outside tending the small garden in front of the church. He heard the phone, got up from his begonias, and walked inside.

The caller ID that Otto had installed to try and avoid the sob stories of weepy parishioners told him who was calling. He answered.

"How ya been, Pie Face?"

"How did you know it was me?"

"All things are known to those who serve."

"Whatever," Pie Face sighed. "Look, I've got a problem. It's pretty bad. I need you to pray for a couple of friends of mine."

"And you'll make your contribution payable to the Ascending Spirit Church of Benton, Louisiana?"

"I know the drill. Their names and descriptions in a separate envelope, right?"

"You're a sharp one. Now, don't worry. It's funny how things work out for believers."

TWENTY-FIVE

RELIABLE SOURCES

Toke sank into the marshmallow softness of his worn easy chair, which was the only piece of even remotely comfortable furniture in his apartment. He flipped on the television, filling the tiny living room with the urgent mutterings of local station WKLR's eleven o'clock news broadcast.

WKLR's signal originated from a small adobe in northern Mingo County that had once been a mission. The message now being spread from inside the building's crumbling walls was vastly different from the one taken forth by the holy men who had built it. In a mad scramble to find a broadcasting niche, the owners of the upstart station had chosen to go with tabloid programming, the content of which catered primarily to those possessed of the most pliant character.

It was the only station Toke watched regularly, and he especially liked the late-edition news. The anchor, Betty Sopol, was a disgraced beauty queen who had been stripped of her crown as Ms. Mingo County 1990 after a series of nude photos, taken by a boyfriend in high school, began showing up for sale at area truck stops. Toke had an enlargement of one of the photos hanging in the men's room at the garage, and he never missed one of Betty's broadcasts.

The camera zoomed in for a tight shot as Betty's heavily made up blue eyes zeroed in on the teleprompter. "A reward of fifty thousand dollars is being offered for information leading to the arrest of the person responsible for last week's robbery of the Bottleneck Savings and Loan," she snapped off, clipping the words to mask her drawl.

Stu's drawing flashed up on the screen. Toke grunted, leaning forward as Betty continued. "Bottleneck police have apparently chosen to disregard the eyewitness account of a man who claims the bank robber wore a mask like the one seen here. Bottleneck resident Stu Pateman, who is responsible for this rendering, is in the studio with our own Aaron Honeysucker. Aaron?"

The drawing disappeared, replaced by a shot of co-anchor Aaron Honeysucker. He was seated on an emerald green divan in the middle of a set made up to resemble a cozy drawing room. Across the coffee table from him, in the folding metal chair reserved for special guests, sat Stu, who was wearing an ill-fitting white suit and a bolo tie.

"Thank you, Betty," Honeysucker said. He turned to face Stu.

"Mr. Pateman, can you tell our viewers what you saw on the night of the bank robbery?"

"Well," Stu began, fidgeting with his tie, "I was out walking around, minding my own business, when I seen this fella, the one I drew, come crawling out of the bank window. He was carrying what looked to me like a big purse."

"That must have been the moneybag," Honeysucker said to the camera.

"Uh, yeah, I reckon so. Anyway, this fella took off down the alley that runs alongside the bank, and I ran across the street from where I was, trying to get a better look at him. But by the time I got to the alley, I heard a car start up and drive off. It must've been the getaway car."

"And then you went immediately to the police, correct?"

"Well, no, not exactly. By that time I was real tired, y'see, and—"

"You needed some time to mull over what you had just seen."

"Something like that. But I did go to the police the next morning, and it didn't have nothing to do with the reward. I didn't even know about the reward until I got there and they told me about it."

"You were just trying to do your civic duty," Honeysucker said, "and the police, they treated your story with disdain?"

"They treated me like a damn idiot, if that's what you mean. Made some crack about a spider robbing the bank, or something like that, and tried to say I was making the whole thing up for the money."

"That's outrageous."

"What the hell else you gonna expect? The cops ain't got no use for an old boy like me."

"Obviously not. Thank you for coming on, Mr. Pateman."

"Sure thing," Stu said.

The drawing once again filled the screen, along with a text box containing the words "Editorial Opinion." After a few seconds, the image of the mask dissolved, leaving the text box floating beneath Honeysucker's head. He had moved to the news desk, where he was now seated beside Betty.

"One can only wonder at Chief Franklin Dykes's reasoning in disregarding a clue as invaluable as the one provided by Mr. Pateman," he read from a sheet of light blue paper. "Perhaps his department is so on top of things as to need no help from a concerned community. If that's the case, we can all expect them to solve this crime quickly. I suspect, however, that this is not the case. In fact, I'd say the odds of that are roughly the same as those of Chief Dykes learning to smoke a pipe with his rear end."

"Thank you, Aaron," Betty said, chuckling as she turned to the camera. "We will now leave you with another look at the rendering provided to us by Mr. Pateman."

The drawing again filled the screen. Toke stared at it, imagining a stubby forefinger and thumb wriggling from its eyeholes.

"I've seen that mask. I've seen it, and I know where I've seen it," he mumbled. When the station cut to commercial, he got up from his chair and walked into the kitchen, where he hoped to find something to write with.

TWENTY-SIX

TALKING SHOP

Desmond knocked on Chief Dykes's door. When there was no answer, he entered and found Bottleneck's last line of defense against jaywalkers and weekend drunks asleep, his feet propped up on his desk and an issue of *Sportsman's Paradise* folded across his stomach. Desmond turned and pounded on the door loudly. Dykes snapped back to the land of the living.

"You ever hear of knocking?" he grumbled.

"I did knock," Desmond said, taking a seat in front of the chief's desk. "That's why you're awake."

Dykes hoisted himself from his chair, tossed the magazine onto his desk, and walked heavily over to the coffee pot. Unable to find a clean styrofoam cup, he took one from the wastebasket, licked his index finger, and began swabbing out the residue.

"Skeeter told me you'd have a little free time this afternoon," Desmond said.

"Skeeter's got a big mouth," Dykes said, filling his cup. He took a sip, leaned down, and began sifting through the wastebasket. "You want a cup? There's a couple of empties in here that ain't too bad."

"No thanks. I've got some news for you."

"Let me have the good parts first. I ain't quite awake yet."

"I didn't say any of it was good."

Dykes sat down behind his desk and nodded. "Start talking."

"I'm not sure we're on the right track with Kindel. I'm not sure we're on the wrong track either. I'm just not sure."

"So you're not sure."

"No."

"If it's the fingerprints, he could've worn gloves. You know that."

"It's something else. I, uh, took a look around the inside of his place yesterday."

"Without any kind of paper?"

"Yeah."

"And you didn't find any of the money from the bank. You know that doesn't mean he's clean."

"No, he's not clean. I just don't know if he needed the money bad enough to hit the bank. Him and his partner look to be moving enough cocaine through their place to get half this town high."

"He's dealing? Here?"

"He's got more than he needs to party with."

Dykes set his coffee down and began shuffling through the piles of loose paper littering his desk. "I've got something here for you."

"What?"

"Here it is," Dykes said, locating a small, tattered scrap of paper. "Goolsby ran that tag number for you, the one he got off the Mustang that's been parked out at Kindel's. The car's registered to a Cecil Keating. He ain't got any criminal record."

"Not yet."

"Right. We'll watch those two a while longer, then go down there and get them."

"What about probable cause?"

"We'll probably find a cause once we're in there. Know what I mean? Hell, we'll clean them out as soon as Carter gets back in town. We'll need everybody."

Desmond nodded. "That's another thing I wanted to talk to you about. Carter."

"What about him?"

"How close are the two of you?"

"Close enough, I guess. Why are you asking?"

"It's just that . . . well, I guess he just doesn't seem all that dedicated. He's never been thrilled with the surveillance on Kindel."

"Neither have I, to tell you the truth."

"Is he a good cop?"

"Yeah, he is, and I think I know what's bothering you. Carter's got some problems. A little while back, he walked in on a convenience store robbery just outside of town here. He drew down on a fella who'd just escaped from a work farm and killed him. Trouble is, the fella got off a shot, which went clean through Carter and killed the store's owner. Old boy named Billy Hotard, lived here all his life."

"Jesus."

"Yeah, and keep in mind Carter'd only been on the job a few months at the time. Hadn't seen any action—not that there's ever that much to see around here—but he was raw, y'know. And to top it off, we'd just gotten a couple of these flak jackets for the boys to wear out on patrol, and Carter was supposed to be wearing one when that slug went through him and killed Hotard. It did a real number on his head, so if he don't seem all that enthusiastic right now, that's why."

"Should he even be working?"

"Not according to a shrink we had come in and look at him. Said he was stressed out or something. That vacation he was on when you got here was sort of forced."

"Then why isn't he still on vacation?"

"Hell, I've only got three men here. The bank gets robbed, which hasn't happened in forever as far as I know, and then you come breezing into town. I had to have somebody to babysit you, and I thought Carter would be best for it, scrambled head or not. I didn't think it'd be all that hard a job, and hell, it's just stress. It's not like he's ready for the nut hatch or anything like that."

"I guess that explains things. A little."

TWENTY-SEVEN

A SOFTER LANDING

That's the most money I've ever seen at one time in my life," Enid said. She was standing in her kitchen, peering into the paper sack full of cash that Carter had just handed her. Cliff, who was eating an apple, walked over and looked inside.

"Where'd you get it?" he asked.

"Playing cards," Carter said, sitting down at the table and pulling the tab from a can of beer. He took a swig. "I'm in a running poker game with some of the guys at the station."

"That's one hell of a winning streak you've been on," Cliff said, biting into his apple and grinning. "Mind if I rub you for luck?"

"Don't touch me, Cliff."

"Shut up, you two," Enid said. She folded the bag and walked over to the refrigerator. She opened the freezer, took out a package of hamburger meat, and placed the money inside.

"Why're you freezing the money, Ma?" Cliff stammered.

"I'm gonna thaw this meat for dinner. Why don't you run to the store and get me a pack of buns, Cliff. Get the money out of my purse."

"All right. C'mon, Carter."

"I wanna talk to Carter. Go by yourself."

Cliff shrugged and exited the kitchen as Enid took the meat to the sink and began running a stream of warm water over it. "Where in Heaven's name did you get that money, Carter?"

"I told you."

"I know you're a good boy. You always were. But if you inherited even just a little bit of this family's luck, I don't see how you could have won that money playing a card game. And even if you did, you know I don't think much of gambling."

"Use the money, Enid. Take Lonnie and put him in that home when he needs to go."

Enid leaned against the counter. "He's going down so fast now, Carter."

"And there's nothing we can do about it," Carter said. "But maybe this way he won't have to land so hard."

TWENTY-EIGHT

SPECIAL DELIVERY

Toke gunned Carter's truck over the last few miles of high-way leading out to Dakota's. The huge vehicle's chassis groaned menacingly and the cab began to vibrate as the speedometer reached sixty.

It had been a long time since anything resembling a plan of action had taken shape in Toke's mind. Most of his adult life had been spent drifting from one disastrous bungle to the next with hardly a glance toward the future, but he now saw an opportunity to put those days behind him.

He pulled one hand away from the steering wheel and placed it over his shirt pocket, patting the folded motor oil invoice inside. He had worked painfully through several drafts before settling on the final version of the extortion letter he had scribbled on the back of it.

He zipped past the airstrip without slowing down, then broke hard and swerved into Dakota's driveway. The truck's tires sprayed an arc of gravel and dirt across the yard as he cut the wheel and skidded to a halt beside his T-bird, which was parked in front of Dakota's trailer.

As Toke got out of the truck and walked around to the front of the T-bird, Dakota emerged from the trailer clothed in an oversized bathrobe.

"What are you doing barreling up in here like that, you idiot?" she screamed. "Are you stoned?"

Toke looked Dakota up and down, leaning back against the hood of the car. "Where's your boyfriend?"

"If you mean Carter, he's not around. He went to see some relatives."

"Damn. His buddies at the station said he had the day off. I thought I might find him out here."

"What do you want, Wheeler?"

Toke held up the keys to Carter's truck, jingled them, and tossed them to Dakota. She caught them with one hand.

"Just wanted to bring him his truck," Toke said. "What's he driving, by the way?"

"My truck. He didn't think that hunk of rust you loaned him would make the trip."

Toke looked hurt. He walked around to the driver's side of the car and poked his head in the open window. The keys were in the ignition. "You ought not talk about my baby that way."

He walked up to Dakota, taking the invoice from his pocket and handing it to her. "Give this to your boy, will ya?"

Dakota took the invoice from Toke with a smirk.

"You can look it over if you want. Y'know, check my spelling."

She unfolded it and looked it over. "He buy some oil from you or something?"

"Read the other side."

Dakota turned the invoice over and read Toke's uneven scrawl.

Dear Cop,

If you don't want Chief Dikes to know his favorite deputy's been moonliting as a bank robber, let's you and me make a deal. I'm easy on the split.

"What the hell is this?"

"Can't you read good, girl?"

"You're nuts," Dakota said. She balled the invoice up and tossed it at Toke. It bounced off his face and landed at his feet. "Give it to him yourself."

"No, I don't think he likes me much," Toke said, walking back to the T-bird. "I'll let you give it to him. Tell him he can give me a call if he wants to talk about it. Somehow, I think he will."

Toke got into the car, started it, and drove off. Dakota watched him leave, then picked up the invoice. She un-balled it and read it again.

TWENTY-NINE

WORKING AROUND THE EDGES

Dakota sat on her couch clipping grocery coupons from the back pages of the *Mingo County Times* with a pair of dull scissors. She had mangled most of the coupons so badly that she wondered whether or not the checkout girls at the store would even accept them. Now she was very carefully working her way around the edges of one that offered a seventy-five cent savings on her son Brian's favorite breakfast cereal. He would be visiting for his birthday soon, and she wanted to make sure the kitchen was well stocked.

She heard the sound of a car churning the gravel outside and looked out the window as the twin beams from the headlights crept across the yard, illuminating for a moment a malnourished-looking cat that was picking its way through her garbage. The cat froze in the lights. As the beams moved past it, Dakota saw the animal make its way toward the woods, a half-eaten chicken breast clutched in its teeth. Dakota hoped it didn't choke on one of the bones as she watched Carter get out of her truck and walk toward the trailer. She set her coupons and scissors carefully to the side.

Carter knocked lightly and entered. "Honey, I'm home," he said, smiling.

"How was your trip?"

"Fine. Thanks for letting me use the truck."

"And your uncle?"

"He's all right. As good as can be expected. How'd my truck get here?"

"Toke Wheeler brought it out."

"That was mighty white of him," Carter said as he walked over and sat down on Dakota's right, picking up her coupon clipping paraphernalia and setting it gingerly on the coffee table.

"Your truck wasn't all he brought," Dakota said. She reached under the sofa cushion to her left and withdrew the crumpled invoice. She extended it to Carter, who had begun fiddling with the remote.

"What's this?" he said distractedly as he flipped on the TV. He tossed the remote onto the table and took the invoice from Dakota. "I didn't buy any oil from that guy."

"The other side."

Carter flipped the invoice and began reading, his mouth dropping slightly open.

"What does it mean, Carter?"

"Nothing," Carter said, getting up from the couch and walking into the kitchenette. "Have you got anything to drink here?"

"In the cabinet over the stove."

Carter opened the cabinet and took out a half-empty bottle of bourbon. He unscrewed the cap and poured three inches of the whiskey into a plastic cup, downing half of it in one gulp.

"Carter," Dakota said, grabbing the remote and turning off the TV, "I don't want to pry, but is it something to do with the bank in town getting robbed? Is it that?"

"You're not prying. Look, Dakota, I can't talk to you about this right now. I like you a lot, and I know that keeping secrets isn't any way to start a relationship, but I can't talk about it."

"All right."

"I think I should go," Carter said, downing the rest of the bourbon.

"No, I want you to stay."

"You sure?"

"I'm sure."

"Okay," Carter said, nodding. "I'm gonna go in the back and get some sleep." He placed the plastic cup in the sink and headed for the bedroom.

Dakota took the paper from the table and went back to work on the cereal coupon. She cut slowly, biting her tongue as she went.

THIRTY

THE BOTTOM OF THINGS

Desmond's car was parked on the side of the highway, a few hundred yards north of Dakota's trailer. He sat behind the wheel and watched the driveway through his binoculars, waiting for Carter to emerge from the trailer and drive south toward town. He hoped Carter drove south. It would be hard to explain what he was doing hanging out on the side of the highway at seven o'clock in the morning.

Desmond had stayed up all night sketching and thinking about how to approach Dakota. He knew she was mixed up with Keating and Kindel somehow, but he hadn't been able to figure out the nature of the connection. In a small town like Bottleneck, everybody knew everybody. She may have gone to school with one of them, or maybe that mechanic of hers did and she knew the dealers through him.

Just getting a little crazy at a party Desmond could handle. As far as he was concerned, the drug use was her own business. Everybody made mistakes. But if the girl knew Kindel and his pal were up to something illegal, it complicated things considerably, especially in regard to Carter.

Desmond liked Carter, and he felt slightly guilty about not telling him what he had found under Kindel's bed—at least the part about the drugs. He wouldn't have had any idea how to broach the topic of Dakota's little video.

He had so far suppressed his feelings of dishonesty by going back to Carter's pissing and moaning about staking out Kindel's place. It was damn strange. He was sure Carter was hiding something, and he wanted to know what that something was before he and the police moved to take Kindel down.

From what Dykes had told him, he thought Carter's secret probably had something to do with his not wanting anybody to think he was half out of his mind. That's what Desmond was hoping.

Taking his cup of rapidly cooling coffee from the dash, Desmond rolled down the window and tossed the dark liquid out. It caused a column of steam to rise from the chilled earth. He stared at this as he tossed the empty cup onto the seat beside him. When he looked back at the trailer, there was exhaust billowing from the tailpipe of Carter's truck. The brake lights came on, then flickered as the truck backed up, turned, and rolled forward. Carter paused where the driveway met the road, then pulled off, heading south.

As soon as Carter was out of sight, Dakota came out, got into her truck, and drove quickly toward the airstrip. Desmond followed.

～

Stepping into the hangar, Desmond heard the clang of metal on metal. Dakota stood beside her plane, absent-mindedly tapping one of the wing flaps with a small hammer and cursing beneath her breath.

"Does Carter know you're a junkie?" Desmond asked. He shoved his hands into his pockets and put on his sternest face.

Dakota whirled. "What?"

"Your drug problem. Is Carter aware of it?"

Dakota threw the hammer. It whizzed by Desmond's head and smacked against the wall of the hangar, leaving a small dent.

"I don't know whether to interpret that as a yes or a no. Help me out."

"What the hell are you doing here?"

"Working on a case."

"I'm not any part of your damn case," Dakota said. She turned and stormed into the hangar's walk-in storage closet, slamming the door behind her.

Desmond walked over and tried the door, but it was locked. "Open up, Dakota. We need to talk."

"Go to hell!" she screamed from behind the door.

"Look, I'm sorry I started off that way."

"That makes two of us!"

Desmond let go of the knob and dropped his hands to his sides. "I was in Kindel's place the other day. I saw the tape, Dakota. I know about you and them, about you and the drugs."

He could hear her rummaging around, and the thought crossed his mind that she might have a gun in there. After a minute, the door swung open, and Dakota emerged with a large wrench in her hand.

Desmond took a quick step back. "What are you planning to do with that?"

"Tighten a nut," she said, walking past him and over to the plane. "So you've got the tape, huh? What're you going to do with it?"

"I don't have it; I left it there. I didn't have a warrant. And as far as what I'm going to do with it, that's up to you. I'm only interested in nailing Kindel and Keating."

"I have a son. Did you know that?"

"No."

"He has a father who'd love to have a reason to take him away."

"What's your connection to those two?"

"I don't have one. Horace does. He's the one who shot the tape that night at the party, when things got so crazy."

"Why?"

"They need my plane to fly the drugs up from someplace in Mexico. Horace says that if I don't keep letting them use it, he'll mail a copy of the tape to my ex and to the principal at my son's school. I'm not involved in it, I don't get any money from it, I just get to keep custody of my kid."

Desmond walked over to the plane. He leaned against the wing, stroking it. "Can a plane like this fly all the way to Mexico and back without stopping? It doesn't seem to me like it could."

"It can't. Horace stops on his way back and refuels outside a place called Tarpole Flats, just north of the border. There's a little strip west of the town."

"So Horace flies the plane?"

"Yeah."

"And Carter is aware of how much of this?"

"None of it. I thought maybe Carter could help me, but he's got problems of his own."

"So you're using him."

"Maybe at first I thought I would, thought I could. But not now. It isn't that way at all."

"Guess it's none of my business."

"No."

"Well, this isn't any of my business either, but how long have you been using?"

"A while now. Off and on. Who else has seen that tape?"

"Nobody."

"What are you going to do with it?"

"I don't think it's an important part of my investigation. It will probably end up being erased at some point."

"Thanks."

"When will Horace be going back to Tarpole Flats?"

"He's asked me if he can use the plane tomorrow. He'll leave early in the morning."

"Not much time."

"You gonna arrest him?"

Desmond nodded. "I'd definitely start looking for a new mechanic."

THIRTY-ONE

THE SITUATION

W hat do you mean his horse got out?" Carter asked. He
was standing in front of Skeeter's desk, quizzing him
about Chief Dykes's whereabouts. "I thought that old nag of
his got struck by lightning during that storm last month."

"That's what everybody thought at first," Skeeter said.
"Turns out, she only fainted. The vet says she's got a weak
heart. Wormy or something. Anyway, Goolsby's out there
right now trying to help him get her back in the corral."

"Oh."

"You ever see how they do it?"

"No," Carter said. He walked over and plopped down on
the bench, crossing his legs and fiddling with his shoelace.

"Goolsby takes a bucket of oats and tries to lure the horse
into the corral while the chief sits in his car and watches,"
Skeeter said, starting to chuckle. "It's pretty funny."

"Sounds hilarious. I don't guess Desmond's out there with
them."

"Not that I know of," Skeeter said, returning to his reading.

As was his custom on Wednesdays, which were normally slow, he had pulled a batch of old files that morning to keep himself entertained. He was in the middle of one that detailed the case of an elderly man who had killed his roommate with a broken whiskey bottle after getting into an argument with the younger man over the last drink.

The killer, Silas "Fats" Gerard, had broken the bottle over his roommate's head and then plunged its splintered remains repeatedly into the prostrate man's neck. After the killing, he walked to the corner liquor store, took a bottle of Rebel Yell from the shelf without paying for it, and swilled the whiskey as he made his way to the police station, where he calmly turned himself in and slurred a confession. Skeeter had scrawled the confession on a napkin he had been using to wipe chicken grease from his fingers, locked the man up, and walked with Carter over to the boarding house the men lived in to survey the carnage.

"Hey, Carter, remember that call we went out on your first week here?"

"I seem to recall there being more than one, Skeeter."

"Yeah, you're right. But I'm talking about that tubby old queer who cut his boyfriend up with a whiskey bottle over at old lady Durant's boarding house. You've got to remember that one."

Carter got up from the bench and walked over to the water fountain. "Yeah, I remember it," he said, pushing the button and touching his lips to the weak stream of water that oozed from the spout. "That the file on it?"

"Yep. 'Bout the worst thing we've ever seen around here."

"Yeah, and I'd just about forgotten it. Thanks for reminding me. That's a morbid-ass hobby you've got."

Goolsby burst into the station. His uniform was covered in

mud and torn in several places. There was blood trickling from behind his left ear, and that entire side of his face was bruised.

"What the hell happened to you?" Skeeter asked, getting up from behind his desk and walking over to Goolsby. "Where's the chief?"

"He's right behind me. He made me throw a rope around that damn horse after she wouldn't follow me and the bucket of oats into the corral. That fucking nag. You know she hasn't more than trotted since he bought her, but she took off like a shot the second the rope was around her neck. I got it tangled around my wrist, and she drug me all over that place."

"What happened to your head?" Carter asked.

"Hit it on a tree stump." Goolsby wiped the blood from behind his ear and looked at it. "Damn," he said, wiping his hand on his pants.

Dykes entered the station, looked at Goolsby, and shook his head. "I owe you one, Matt. Whatever you want, just name it."

"How 'bout a couple days off to recover from my injuries?"

"You can have all the time off you want, so long as it starts after tomorrow. Carter, where the hell's your partner?"

"Desmond? I don't know. I thought he'd be here by now."

"Let's wait for him in my office," Dykes said. "There's something serious I need to talk to you all about."

~

"So what's so all-fired important, Chief?" Skeeter asked. "Don't tell me you already learned how to smoke a pipe with your butt."

"Shut the hell up, Skeeter," Dykes grumbled. "You boys

best be getting your game faces on. We've got some business to take care of."

"What kind of business?" Goolsby asked, massaging his ear.

"We'll talk about it when Agent Kyle shows up for work," Dykes said, taking his car keys from his pocket and poking the ignition key into his right ear to scratch.

"Trying to start your head, Chief?" Goolsby asked, then shifted uncomfortably in his chair as Dykes eyed him menacingly.

After several minutes of tense silence, there was a knock at the door, and Desmond stuck his head in. "Sorry I'm late," he said. "Mind if I crash this little party?"

"Hell no," Dykes said. "It's being thrown in your honor."

Desmond walked in and stood beside the chief's desk. "Where do I start?"

"At the beginning'll do. I haven't gotten into it with them."

Desmond laid it out for them. Throughout his briefing, he caught Carter eyeing him with what he interpreted as a mixture of mild anger and befuddlement. When he had finished, he leaned against the wall as Dykes eased himself from behind his desk to address the troops.

"We'll go and roust them out of there tomorrow morning," he said. "So hang loose until then. I don't see any reason to watch them tonight. They ain't going anywhere."

Desmond nodded in agreement.

"Now, there ain't anything in this Kindel's file to indicate he's especially dangerous," Dykes continued. "He used a cap gun in that stickup he pulled, and he gave himself up peaceful enough when the law come for him. As for this friend of his, who knows? He may be crazy as a Betsy bug. Now go out and write some tickets or something."

Desmond grabbed Carter by the arm just outside the chief's office. "Look, Carter, I'm sorry I didn't tell you about finding the dope when I went down to Kindel's place. I just felt like I should let your boss in on it first."

"Don't sweat it."

"You sure? I feel pretty bad about it. We are supposed to be working as partners for as long as this thing lasts."

"Yeah, for as long as it lasts. I'm not mad about it. You did the right thing running it by the chief first."

"I'm glad you understand."

"Sure I do. I'll see you later. I've got some tickets to write."

Desmond watched Carter walk down the hall, then turned and walked back into Dykes's office. "You got body armor for everybody?"

THIRTY-TWO

HOMEMADE SIN

Desmond broke the seal on the half pint of Wild Turkey he had picked up on his way back to the Inn and Out and took a swig straight from the bottle. He wasn't normally much of a drinker, but the day's events had left him craving the chemically induced oblivion and subsequent dreamless sleep a night of unabated boozing promised.

He took another pull from the bottle and set it on the table beside the bed. Picking up the phone, he dialed the number of the FBI office in Austin.

The stern voice of receptionist Celia Bonner came over the line. "You've reached the FBI, how may we help you?"

"Celia? This is Desmond Kyle."

"Hey, Des," Celia said, her voice softening. "What's going on?"

"I'm sitting in a hotel room getting drunk all by myself."

"That's a crying shame. Aren't there any pretty girls down there?"

"It's terrible, Celia. I'm still looking for one with a full set of teeth."

"Are you serious?"

"No," Desmond said, picking up the bottle and taking another drink. "Did Simon and Raoul get my message?"

"Sure did. They left for Tadpole Flats this afternoon."

"Tarpole Flats."

"What?"

"Nothing. I'm sure they'll figure it out."

"What's going on down there, Desmond? Who's this Mackey person?"

"I promise I'll tell you all about it the next time I see you."

Desmond told Celia goodbye and hung up. He set the bottle down, took his sketch pad from beneath the bed, and began a drawing of Horace Mackey. He chuckled as he made Mackey's face the mask of stupefied shock he imagined the smuggler would be wearing when surprised by Simon and Raoul.

THIRTY-THREE

A DOG'S LIFE

The steady rain falling on Bottleneck and most of Mingo County kept Carter from rolling down the driver's side window as he guided his truck slowly along the twisting road leading out to Kindel's place. The cigarette he was puffing had rendered the cab an acrid smokehouse.

His eyes watering, he stubbed the cigarette out in the ashtray and reached across the cab, rolling down the passenger window a few inches and momentarily losing control of the truck in the process. He swerved to the left-hand side of the road and clipped an old mailbox, stenciled on which he could make out the name CRAPPS. He regained control of the truck just as the last wisps of smoke made their escape from the cab, then pulled over to the side of the road to roll up the window. As he leaned across the seat, he saw that the stack of hundreds he had brought along with him was now drenched from the rain splashing in.

He had stopped off at the old Bonebrite trading post earlier and dug up the money, taking out this stack and reburying the rest. Carter thought as he was leaving that the floor of the trading post was beginning to look as if a giant, thieving prairie dog had taken up residence there.

He had been shocked and a little frightened at the ease with which his mind almost unconsciously detailed out the plan he was now in the process of carrying through. He would plant the money from the robbery somewhere at Kindel's place so that it could be found during tomorrow's planned raid. Once it was discovered, the investigation into the bank job would end, leaving him free to deal with Wheeler.

After dwelling on the pros and cons of this course of action all afternoon, he had come to feel a uneasy peace about his decision.

He had been nearly overcome with queasiness when his crime cast suspicion on Kindel, who to all outward appearances was just a good old boy living down a few mistakes. Now, however, he felt absolutely no guilt about causing sentences for robbery to be tacked onto whatever the ex-con and his friend would be given for dealing.

As for Wheeler, Carter had been unable to figure out how the little monkey had connected him with the bank robbery, but if some of the money would shut him up, why not pay him off? That would still leave enough to take care of Lonnie, and maybe he would even use a few thousand for himself, ask Dakota if she wanted to go on a vacation. He'd worked hard enough for his ill-gotten gain. He might as well enjoy a little of it. He was, after all, a criminal.

Carter put the money in his jacket pocket and took in his surroundings. The rain had begun to subside, and he saw that his forced stop had brought him to within a few hundred yards of where Kindel's property began. He took his umbrella from the floor of the truck and started walking.

He thought about Desmond as he jumped the rain-filled ditch that ran alongside the road. Carter had meant what he told Desmond about not blaming him for keeping what he found in Kindel's house a secret. It wasn't as if the few days they had been partnered had established them as confidants.

By the time Carter got to Kindel's place, the rain had stopped completely. He looked at his watch and saw that it was after 2 a.m. His hopes that Kindel and anyone else in the house would be sleeping were dashed when he heard the dull roar of a television set tuned to some sporting event emanating from inside. The roar of the crowd was punctuated every few seconds by a pair of guttural chortles.

Carter approached the house slowly. He had decided on the way out that he would plant the cash in the cab of the broken-down truck he had seen resting in the middle of the garden, but as he neared it, he could see that the weeds surrounding the rusting hulk were growing considerably thicker and taller than they appeared from the ridge. Bound to be a snake or two in that mess, he thought.

Then he saw it. There was an old milk can on the porch that would make the perfect vessel. Carter walked toward the house as quietly as he could, wincing with each squelching footfall. He stepped softly onto the porch, expecting its boards to creak, but the old oak was solid.

He tiptoed over and dropped the money into the milk can, then stepped off the porch, congratulating himself on a job stealthily done. It was at this point that Carter became subject to the total Mort experience, smelling the wet fur, hearing the labored breathing, and feeling a nauseating combination of fear and revulsion as he whirled to see the huge dog creep from beneath the porch.

Mort tried to bark, but only a weak moan made its way

past his flabby lips. He tried again, this time coughing violently and flopping to the ground in the throes of a writhing spasm. Carter looked on, transfixed as the dog shuddered grotesquely for several seconds, then lay still.

Trembling with horror, he turned and ran as fast as he could toward the road.

THIRTY-FOUR

A LITTLE PINK IN THE MIDDLE

Floyd and Murray Stimage, who worked for Pie Face Erikson, sat in Floyd's Pontiac Bonneville, sharing a bag of boiled peanuts they had purchased from a roadside vendor. The Bonneville was parked atop a bluff overlooking the Borderline Airstrip just outside Tarpole Flats, Texas.

Horace Mackey, whom Floyd and Murray had come to Tarpole Flats to murder, had just landed his plane and entered The Flyburger, the small café that Dupree Morris, the airstrip's proprietor, ran on the side.

Floyd pulled a handful of goobers from the bag, shelled one, and tossed the nut's soft fruit into his mouth, smacking greedily. "Why the hell didn't Pie Face just grease this guy in Mexico?"

"He's on thin ice with the federales down there," Murray said, "ever since he shot the local chief's dog for chasing that cat of his up a tree. Last thing he needs now is a dead gringo stinking up the scene."

"That makes sense, but didn't he let the guy pick up a shipment?"

"Yeah, a shipment of flour. Pie Face said this clown would be too fucking stupid to check the stuff, and damned if he wasn't right."

"I see," Floyd said. "Well, let's drive on down and take care of business."

"We'll give it a few more minutes. We ain't out of peanuts yet."

Inside the café, Horace stood bellied up to the counter. He had been looking forward to making this trip for Doty and Cecil. It wasn't The Flyburger's food, which was terrible, or a tankful of the Borderline's airplane fuel, which Horace suspected of being cut with water, that he had been eagerly anticipating. It was another opportunity to see Tamara Morris, Dupree Morris's daughter, whom Horace considered the finest woman he had ever laid eyes on.

Tamara was working the grill, her back to Horace. He was enjoying the view.

"How's that burger coming?" Horace asked, imagining what it would be like trying to remove Tamara's tight cutoffs with his teeth.

"It's about there," Tamara replied, flipping the patty and flattening it with her spatula. "Hold your horses."

"Don't burn that meat now. I like it a little pink in the middle."

Horace turned and looked out the café's front window at Dakota's plane, which he had taxied up next to the airstrip's only fuel pump. Dupree had attached the pump's hose to the underside of the plane's fuselage and was now monitoring the refueling.

As Horace looked on, Dupree took a thin cigar from his breast pocket and lit it, tossing the match to the ground dangerously close to a clump of moist sand, where fuel dripping from the hose's rusting nozzle was accumulating.

Shaking his head in disbelief, Horace turned his attention back to Tamara.

"What's a pretty girl like you do for fun around here?" he asked. "Y'all got a honky-tonk or anything like that?"

"Yeah, there's one up the road a ways," Tamara said, turning to face Horace, "and there's plenty to do besides that if you use your imagination."

"Imagination's important, you know it? A lot of people—and it's sad—but a hell of a lot of people never see what ain't right in front of their faces. I know somebody like that up in Bottleneck, a friend of mine named Doty. If you don't draw Doty a picture of something, he can't see it."

"Sounds like your friend ought to jump-start his imagination. There's all kinds of ways of doing it. Does he ever read?"

"I don't know if he can."

"That's what I do. I read. Want to see what I'm reading now?"

"Sure."

Tamara took a tattered paperback from her purse and handed it to Horace. The book, which was entitled *It Takes A Lot*, had on its cover a half-naked peasant woman seemingly melting in the arms of a hulking, shirtless knight.

"You like this kind of stuff?" Horace asked, handing the book back to Tamara.

"Sure. Like I said, it gets me thinking." Tamara turned and scooped Horace's burger from the grill. She slapped it between two buns, dropped it onto a plate, and set it in front of him.

Horace picked up the burger and took a bite. It was like charcoal. Chewing grudgingly, he turned and looked out the window. Dupree was nowhere in sight. The pump, however, was still running, and the plane's tank was now overflowing.

"What the fuck?" he mumbled, spitting the partially chewed clump of burger into his napkin and handing the wad to Tamara. "Where the hell'd your daddy go?"

"Beats me," she said, frowning as she tossed the napkin into the garbage can. "I've never seen him leave the pump running like that."

Exiting the café, Horace jogged over to the fuel pump and switched it off. As he removed the nozzle from the plane, it became detached from the hose, causing the fuel that had stalled there after the pump was switched off to rush out quickly and drench him.

"Shit!" he screamed, throwing the spent hose to the ground and shaking like a wet dog. He took a step back toward the cafe and looked up, freezing in his tracks.

Dupree stood just to the side of the café, a semiautomatic pistol pressed into his temple. Attached to the pistol, wearing a blue knit shirt and a pair of white trousers, was Special Agent Raoul Espargoza. His partner, Simon Nash, was walking towards Horace, his gun drawn.

"Grab some sky, hairbag," Simon said, levelling the weapon at Horace.

Horace spun around and bolted for the plane, moving faster than he had in over a decade. The anterior cruciate ligament in his left knee, understandably surprised by the sudden call to active duty, snapped like an old rubber band.

Falling forward, Horace saw the still-smoking cheroot, which Dupree had dropped when surprised by Simon and Raoul, just before he flopped onto it. His fuel-soaked coveralls ignited instantly.

Raoul shoved Dupree to the ground and rushed to Simon's side. "What the fuck's going on?" he shouted.

The two of them watched as Horace, who was rapidly becoming a human torch, got to his feet and staggered toward the plane. He got the door open and climbed into the cockpit. The plane's engine started, and it began rolling forward slowly. Through the flames that were now engulfing the plane's interior, Simon and Raoul could make out Horace's form as he lurched forward, succumbing to the intense heat. As his head bounced off the control panel, the plane picked up speed and hurtled into Dupree's Cadillac. It exploded on impact, sending hunks of scorched metal flying in all directions.

"Way to go, fuck-up," Raoul berated Simon as the two of them watched the plane and car burn. "Desmond's really gonna be pissed."

"What the hell did I do? The motherfucker just burst into flames."

Tamara had come out of the café and now stood beside Dupree watching the agents haggle. She burst into tears.

On the bluff, Floyd reached into the sack for another peanut. He groped around for several seconds before realizing that he and his brother had gobbled up the last of the soggy treats while watching the fireworks below.

"Damn," he said, his eyes glued to the flaming disaster. "That was one hell of a show."

"Better than a movie," Murray agreed.

THIRTY-FIVE

THE CRUCIFIXER

Edgar Otto had at one time been the highest paid and most feared freelance contract killer in the southwestern United States. In his salad days, his reputation was that of a ruthless assassin who always hit his target and who took pride in carrying out his assignments in a quick, efficient manner that drew no undue attention to himself or his clients. These traits made him a favorite in underworld circles and also the preferred regional operative of various government agencies that required such services.

Edgar's proficiency led to his becoming something of a celebrity. He was invited to parties, weddings, any function at which those he worked for wanted to impress their friends and associates. It became a badge of honor for many mob bosses to have someone as accomplished and feared as Edgar Otto show up and swap stories at their hoodlum-ridden get-togethers. Even some of those viewed by the community at large as respectable civil servants, not to be outdone, would occasionally sneak him in a back door to parade before guests.

Although Edgar was at first leery of the dim spotlight chasing him from event to event, he soon became caught up in the excitement his appearances generated. He knew that the fewer people who saw his face the better, but he enjoyed being a star, the center of attention for a change. He justified this by telling himself over and over that his new system of "networking" was no doubt introducing him to scores of future clients. It was good for business.

New clients, however, weren't the only people Edgar was brushing up against. There were also a good number of ambitious killers who aspired to be everything he already was. Seeing the status that Edgar had obviously achieved made these young Turks even hungrier for an opportunity to shine. Naturally, many of them saw the bumping off of the current king of the hill as a quick and easy path to the big time.

So began a period in his life when Edgar Otto walked the earth a hunted man. His pursuers were not cops, or even friends or relatives of the many men he had killed. They were a gaggle of fellow criminals, out to knock off the fastest gun in the underworld in an attempt to make a quick name for themselves.

They had relatively little trouble drawing a bead on their prey. Edgar, whose countenance had for years been seen by very few who would live to recognize him, had been photographed several times at the countless parties he attended, and those photographs were now circulated widely, often with a bullseye etched across them in crayon or marker. His habits and methods were no longer well-kept secrets either, so proudly had he boasted of them whenever he had gotten a little drunk and been encouraged by admirers.

For a while, he dodged his would-be successors rather easily, leaving behind him as he did a trail of bullet-riddled corpses. Still they came, so he took to mutilating the bodies and leaving them as warnings to anyone foolish enough to try stealing his crown by way of execution. If anything, the more viciously he made his point, the more determined the dogs nipping at his heels became, and there seemed to be a never-ending supply of them.

After a year and a half of this, his business was beginning to suffer badly. He was so busy looking over his shoulder and jumping at every sound that he was unable to work effectively, so he decided to seek the help of his employers, criminal and otherwise, in ending the destructive game.

It was then that Edgar learned a great many things about the men who had been paying his bills. It wasn't only that they had turned a blind eye toward their young henchmen's activities of the past eighteen months. That would have been bad enough. But they had actually been encouraging the onslaught through a betting pool they had set up. The cash pot, which by the time Edgar decided to seek help was rumored to be in the tens of millions, was being fed by practically everyone he had ever worked for, all of whom were hoping that one of their employees would drop the hammer on Edgar and collect. In that event, not only would the victorious organization be due a valuable windfall of operating capital, but also a great deal of much-sought-after prestige.

Edgar was horrified. Through his inveterate social climbing, he had almost literally dug his own grave. He knew without question that his career was over, so he decided to go to ground and at least try and salvage what was left of his life. For years, this was in itself a major task, as killers managed to find him wherever he went. He worked at short-term, seasonal jobs, hooked up with travelling carnivals, everything he could think of to stay on the move and out of sight, but he was constantly sidestepping bullets.

One day, when he had almost given up the ghost, Edgar passed through the town of Benton, Louisiana. He was walking along the road leading through the tiny rural community, trying to hitchhike his way to a month or so of picking oranges in Florida, when he spied a sign in the window of the Ascending Spirit Church that read PASTOR WANTED.

Edgar walked in and took the sign from the window on his way to the church secretary's office. There, he announced that he was a down-on-his-luck country preacher and just the man Benton's holy ascendants, all fifty of them, had been looking for.

To his surprise, everyone bought it. Within a few weeks, he had ingratiated himself to the community, and he even became a passable preacher. It was much easier work than he was used to, and he enjoyed the free time between Sundays, even taking up such carefree hobbies as fishing and whittling to fill the long gaps between his fire-and-brimstone sermons.

After a while, however, he became bored and began taking on odd jobs for various up-and-coming career criminals, people who, because of their superior work ethic and shortage of time in which to plot, he felt would be more trustworthy than his former bosses. He labeled himself the Crucifixer and tendered his services in exchange for generous donations to the Ascending Spirit Ministries.

Two of the people Edgar had come to trust enough to work for were Pie Face Erikson and his partner, Eric Salazar, and it was a job for these drug dealers that had him piloting a rented Ford Tempo along a quiet, south-Texas back road this morning.

He was looking for the home of one Doty Kindel, where he also hoped to find Cecil Keating. The two had been stealing from Pie Face and Eric.

The house was easy to locate. Edgar had asked around

Bottleneck, and the few people who reluctantly admitted to knowing Kindel told him to look for a run-down old place with a pickup truck resting on cinderblocks off to the side of it.

Spotting the landmark, Edgar pulled the Tempo into the driveway and opened its center console, taking out several pamphlets and stuffing them into the inside pocket of his black jacket. As he did so, he fingered the butt of the .380 automatic he was wearing in a shoulder harness.

He got out and walked toward the house, stepping over what appeared to be a freshly dug grave. At the head of the mound was a cracked cinderblock on which someone had scrawled in flesh-tone crayon the word "Mort."

"Idiots," he said as he stepped up onto the porch, took the inspirational literature from his pocket, and knocked hard on the door.

THIRTY-SIX

A LITTLE SHOT OF SALVATION

Cecil pulled himself to a sitting position on the couch, where he had slept, and stared at the test pattern on the TV for several seconds. He looked over at Doty, who was snoring in the recliner.

"Doty, you awake?"

Doty continued snoring. Cecil picked one of his sneakers up from the floor and tossed it at him, bouncing it off his face. Doty woke with a start.

"Hey, you awake?"

"Am now."

"You expecting anybody?" Cecil asked as the knock came again, this time louder.

"No."

"Well, somebody's at the door."

"They probably just wanna read a meter or something. Go answer it."

"I will. You go get your gun, though, in case it's trouble," Cecil said, getting up.

Doty got up and walked into his bedroom as Cecil went to the door. The knock came again and he flung it open. "What're you selling?"

"Salvation, young man, for you and anyone else willing to listen," Edgar said, looking past Cecil for any sign of his partner. He wanted to make sure both of his intended victims were present before getting down to business.

"What the hell are you talking about?"

"I'd like to come in and minister to you," he said, extending his pamphlets. "I'm Reverend Otto, and I've brought good news."

"You're a preacher?" Cecil asked, eyeing the pamphlets as if they might be radioactive.

"That I am." Edgar saw an obese shadow, which he assumed from Pie Face's detailed description to be Doty Kindel, drift into view in the hallway behind Cecil. He reached into his coat and drew out his pistol.

Cecil saw the flash of metal as the nickel-plated automatic cleared its holster. He instinctively thrust his knee into the preacher's groin. This caused the first shot from Edgar's gun, meant to find its mark directly between Cecil's eyes, to drill a tunnel into his lower abdomen. A thick stream of dark blood coursed from the wound as Cecil lurched forward to grapple with his attacker.

"Doty!" he screamed. "Shoot him, Doty!"

In a panic, Doty raised the ancient revolver he had retrieved from his dresser drawer and fired, sending a .38 caliber round into the back of his best friend's head and killing him instantly. Edgar tossed Cecil's limp body aside and straightened himself, smiling as he took aim at Doty and pulled the trigger.

A dull click emanated from the pistol's action. Edgar looked at the gun and saw that the shell casing from the round that had found a home in Cecil's now nonfunctional digestive tract was jammed in the magazine.

Doty fired again, this time hitting his target in the chest. Edgar took two steps into the house, tripped over Cecil's corpse, and fell to the floor, a look of surprise spreading across his face as he drew his last breath.

Doty, breathing heavily and feeling as if he were walking through molasses, trudged over and pushed the door shut. He looked at the bodies, then turned and walked toward his bedroom and the drugs. He needed to get stoned.

THIRTY-SEVEN

MOPPING UP

Carter, Desmond, and the rest of what passed for a SWAT team in Bottleneck were preparing to leave the hunting club, where they had gathered for their final pep talk from Chief Dykes, when Skeeter spotted the gray Tempo pulling into the dealers' driveway.

Thinking that the driver was probably a salesman of some sort, or just someone looking for directions after getting turned around on the back roads spiderwebbing the area, Dykes and Desmond jointly decided to wait until the unexpected visitor left before going down.

The shots ringing up from Kindel's, however, spurred them to action. Carter and Desmond jumped into their car and hit the logging trail, followed by Skeeter, Goolsby and the chief. It took them several minutes to get to the highway and several more to reach Kindel's.

When they arrived, the house, which minutes earlier had sounded like a shooting gallery, was quiet. Desmond took out his pistol and approached the house, Carter following close

138

behind him. Dykes and his deputies drew down on the front door, waiting to see what happened next.

"I'm gonna knock," Desmond said.

"Are you crazy?" Carter hissed. "Just kick the door in."

"You think so?"

"Hell yes I think so. We're not exactly here delivering flowers."

Desmond lunged at the door, knocking it open with his shoulder. He saw the bodies, then Doty, who was sitting on the sofa gazing into a small mountain of cocaine on the table before him. Several empty plastic bags were spread about the room, where he had thrown them in his frenzy to get stoned as quickly as possible.

Doty, confused and half blind from his furious snorting, tried desperately to focus on the intruders. Fearing he was once again under attack, he inched his hand toward the pistol resting next to him on the sofa.

"Don't do it, Kindel," Desmond growled. "Give yourself up."

Doty snatched the gun, took quick aim, and fired at Desmond, hitting him between the third and fourth ribs on his right side and knocking him to the body-littered floor. Desmond's wild volley of return fire peppered the wall behind Doty, but the lone shot Carter squeezed off caught the fat man in the forehead, shearing off the upper quarter of his skull and filling the room with a fine pink mist.

Carter kept his gun trained on Doty's almost headless body for several seconds, until it flopped forward onto the coffee table.

Dykes, Skeeter, and Goolsby burst into the room as Carter was helping Desmond to his feet. The agent fingered his side, pulling the deformed slug from where it had slightly penetrated the bulletproof vest he was wearing.

He winced, tossing the bullet to the chief and patting the vest. "See how handy these things can come in?"

He turned to Carter, who was staring blankly at what was left of Kindel. "You all right?"

Carter nodded.

Dykes shoved the slug into his pocket and looked around at the carnage. "Jesus Christ. This place looks like a morgue."

"Gay love triangle gone sour if I ever saw one, Chief," Goolsby said.

"Yeah, well, whatever," Dykes replied. "We'll sort all that out later. Right now, let's turn this place inside out. It looks like most of the drugs Desmond saw probably just got snorted up, but there might be more hidden around here. Spread out."

"I'll take the back of the house," Desmond snapped, turning on his heel and heading for Doty's bedroom. There he found the strongbox open on the floor. There were still two bags of dope and the tape, which Desmond removed. It was too large for any of his pockets, so he reached behind himself and stuck it into his waistband, where it could rest against the small of his back and be hidden by his jacket.

Hearing a commotion, he walked back into the den, where Goolsby was proudly displaying to his comrades a huge wad of cash.

"I found it in that old milk can out on the porch," he said. "I'll bet it's money from the bank robbery, Chief."

"I'll be damned," Dykes said, turning to Desmond. "Looks like your idea to watch this old boy wasn't so bad after all."

THIRTY-EIGHT

SOMETIMES IT'S HARD TO SWALLOW

Dr. Fritch cut an inch of sauerkraut-laden frankfurter and bun from his hot dog, skewered it, and guided it carefully into his mouth, chewing slowly. He was sitting at a table in Bottleneck's Hot Diggity Deli, where he had come for a bite after finding the police station locked. A note scotch-taped to the front door read CLOSED FOR TAKING CARE OF POLICE BUSINESS. BACK BEFORE LUNCH.

Swallowing, Fritch thrust his left arm forward, freeing his wristwatch from his tweed coat's heavy sleeve. It was 11:47. He looked out the window at the station, which was across the street and several blocks down. Still deserted.

Fritch had swung into town to check up on Carter, who had yet to call his office about setting up a therapy schedule. He hoped Carter hadn't decided to try and work through things on his own. He needed help.

Fritch made a second, surgically precise incision into his hot dog. As he did so, he heard a muffled giggle coming from the direction of the deli counter. He looked up to see the

waitress who had taken his order eyeing him. She was leaning against the counter next to the establishment's only
other customer, a chubby man wearing camouflage overalls
and a bright orange cap. He also seemed amused.

Irritated, Fritch stabbed the bit of hot dog with his fork
and brought it to his lips. When the giggle came again, he
dropped the fork and fixed the laughing pair with his most
virulent stare.

"Just what do the two of you find so funny about me and
this hot dog?" he asked, raising his voice a little more than
he had meant to.

The waitress blushed a bright red and walked around to
the other side of the counter. The chubby man scratched his
chin.

"Sorry, partner," he said. "Sure didn't mean to be inhos-
pitable."

"Well, I'm sorry I snapped like that. It really isn't like me."

"Ain't ever seen anybody eat a hot dog with a fork is all,"
the man explained. "Kind of a finger food, ain't it?"

"Yes, I suppose it is, but I have an extremely narrow esoph-
agus. I have to be very careful not to swallow too much at
once, and cutting my meals into small bites helps me with
that. Understand?"

"Uh-huh."

"Once, when I was a boy, I managed to get a piece of steak
stuck in my throat while dining at a four-star restaurant with
my parents. I was rushed to the emergency room, where the
doctor used a liquid meat tenderizer to dissolve the steak.
You can't imagine what a terrible experience that was."

"I don't get it," the waitress said, bubbly now, eager to
redeem herself. "Why didn't it just tenderize your windpipe?"

"I've often wondered about that myself," Fritch said,

picking up his fork and gobbling down its bounty. "Just lucky, I guess."

The man walked over from the counter and extended his hand. "Mason Kimbrough."

"Bill Fritch," the doctor said, taking Mason's hand and motioning for him to sit down at the table. "Tell me, Mason, is it normal for the police station to be locked up and deserted this time of day?"

"Not that I know of."

"Well, it is."

The waitress walked back around the counter. "All the boys from over there were in here for coffee this morning," she said. "They were talking about some big bust or something. I couldn't help but overhear."

"Was Carter Jackson with them?" Fritch asked.

"Sure was."

Two police cars zoomed past on the street outside the deli. Fritch watched through the window as they skidded to a stop in front of the station. Carter and a man he didn't recognize got out of the first car, while Chief Dykes and two more officers emerged from the second. There was a good deal of back slapping as the five of them walked into the station.

"Nice meeting the two of you," Fritch said, getting up and exiting the deli.

∾

Fritch nearly ran over Goolsby as he burst into the station. He walked past Carter and Desmond, who were seated on the visitors' bench, and stopped at Skeeter's desk.

"Help you, Doc?"

"I need to see Chief Dykes."

"The chief's a little busy right now. What's up?"

Fritch turned and pointed a trembling finger at Carter. "What's up is that this man shouldn't be taking part in this department's field operations. He's not up to it."

"Not up to it?" Skeeter asked incredulously. "Hell, he blew a drug dealer's head clean off this morning."

"Shut the hell up, Skeeter," Carter said.

Dykes emerged from the restroom and spotted Fritch. "Jesus," he muttered.

"Chief, I have a bone to pick with you."

"Save it, Doc," Carter said. He stood up, took his badge from his shirt, and tossed it to Fritch. "Guys, it's been fun."

Carter walked out of the station. Fritch looked down at the badge.

"What in God's name am I supposed to do with this?"

Dykes walked over and put his arm around the doctor's shoulders. "Let me show you."

THIRTY-NINE

A MAN'S GOT NEEDS

Carter picked up the phone and dialed the number that was scrawled across the bottom of Toke's blackmail invoice. He gave it five rings and was just about to drop the receiver into its cradle when the other end picked up. He heard heavy breathing and the sound of a television set blaring in the background.

"Wheeler?" he asked hesitantly, thinking he had dialed the wrong number.

"Who is it?" a voice queried groggily from the earpiece.

"Is this Toke Wheeler?"

"Yeah, it's me. Who the hell am I talking to?"

"This is Carter Jackson. What's the matter with you?"

"Nothing. I just fell asleep watching TV and you kind of woke me up."

"Sorry."

"You ever wake up to the phone ringing, pick it up, and then forget what to say? I mean, you're supposed to say hello, but it can kind of slip your mind when somebody catches you off guard."

"Look, I'm calling about this note you left with Dakota. What do you want?"

"I thought it was pretty self-explanatory," Toke replied, taking on as haughty a tone as he was capable of. "Either you give me some of that money you took out of the bank, or I'll call the chief down on you."

"What makes you think he'd believe you?"

"Could be he'd laugh in my face. Could be everybody would. But if you don't come across with that cash, we'll find out, and I don't think you can risk it."

"Why are you doing this, Toke?"

"Same reason you knocked over the bank, I imagine. A man's got needs."

"If you ever come near Dakota again, I'm gonna kill you."

"That's fair enough."

"You know where the old Bonebrite trading post is?"

"I've lived here all my life."

"Well, meet me there tomorrow morning, pretty early."

"Why?"

"Just be there. You'll get your money."

Carter slammed the receiver down. There was a knock at the door. He got up to answer it, but before he could make it over, Cliff came tripping in, followed by Enid.

"Hey, cuz," Cliff said. "Surprised to see us?"

"Uh, yeah. Actually I am. What are y'all doing here?"

"Just checking up on you," Enid said, patting Carter on the arm as she walked past him and entered the kitchen. He heard her open the refrigerator and begin rifling through its contents.

"Didn't you two have to work today?" Carter asked Cliff.

"Not for long. Half an hour after shift change this morning, a big rotor blade broke off a turbine and cut this new guy clean in half."

"Jesus."

"Watch that language!" Enid yelled from the kitchen.

"It was bad," Cliff continued. "They shut the plant down, gave everybody the rest of the day off. Ma wanted to drop in on you. She's got it in her head you ain't been taking care of yourself."

"And I sure was right," Enid said, walking in from the kitchen. "There's nothing in that icebox to stick to a man's bones."

"Yeah, Ma," Cliff said. "You can tell he ain't been eating right. Looks like a family of Chinamen moved out of the seat of his pants."

"Well, we can fix that," Enid said, turning to Carter.

"What's that good catfish place we ate at last time me and Cliff came over?"

"Ma's Pantry. They've got chicken, too."

"We'll decide when we get there," Cliff said. "Let's hit the road."

≈

Ma's was packed. When a table finally freed up, Enid and Cliff made a beeline for it as Carter detoured toward the jukebox.

"I'm going to drop a few quarters into this thing," he said. "Order me some fish."

He perused the selections for a moment, dropped his change into the slot, and was programming his choices when he noticed Desmond, who was seated at a table near the men's room, staring at him.

"Hey, man," Carter said. "Who tipped you off about this place."

"Skeeter," Desmond said. "I got tired of eating in my hotel

room. Didn't really expect to see you out after what happened today."

"My aunt and cousin showed up out of the blue, wanted to take me out and fatten me up. You by yourself?"

Desmond nodded.

"Well, come over and eat with us."

"I don't want to intrude on your get-together."

"You won't be intruding. Just don't mention anything about me quitting the force. They've already got all they need to worry about."

"Deal," Desmond said, picking up his plate and following Carter over to the table where Enid and Cliff were seated.

Carter made the introductions. He, Enid and Cliff watched Desmond eat until their own food arrived. The four of them ate quietly until Enid spoke up.

"Carter, I called to check in on Lonnie last night."

"How's he doing?"

"The nurse I talked to said he was adjusting to his surroundings real well, quicker than most of their patients do."

"Who's Lonnie?" Desmond asked.

"An uncle of mine," Carter said. "We had to put him in a home."

"Best place in Texas," Cliff said. "Most expensive, too. Cost an arm and a leg, but we swung it thanks to Carter."

"Really?" Desmond asked.

"Yep. Craziest thing I've ever seen. One day the boy's poor as a church mouse, and the next day he's got money falling out of his ass."

"Cliff!" Enid gasped. "Watch your filthy mouth. And stop all that talk about money. I raised you better than that."

"It's pretty tacky, Cliff," Carter said.

"Sorry. But let me warn you, Mr. Kyle, don't ever play

cards with this boy. I'm surprised the fellas at the station'll even talk to him after the way he's been cleaning them out."

Desmond looked at Carter, who suddenly seemed to find his catfish especially interesting.

Once everyone had finished, Carter pushed his plate away and stood.

"We best be going," he said to Enid. "You and Cliff have a long drive back."

"Nice meeting you, Mr. Kyle," Enid said as she and Cliff rose to leave.

"I enjoyed it," he replied. "You two be careful on the road."

As they made their way toward the door, Carter turned back to Desmond. "Don't leave town without saying good-bye, all right?"

"I wouldn't dream of it." Desmond watched them leave. He sipped at his beer, trying to recall any mention around the station of a card game at which Carter had made out like a bandit.

It certainly seemed like the kind of thing that would come up, even amid all the recent excitement.

A waitress came over and began clearing off the table. When she reached for Carter's beer bottle, Desmond grabbed her arm.

"Don't touch that one," he said, releasing the girl and taking a plastic evidence bag from his coat pocket. Carefully, he picked the bottle up by its lip and dropped it into the bag.

"You some kind of collector or something?" the girl asked. "'Cause if you are, my boyfriend's got an unopened six-pack of Billy Beer he'll sell you. Ought to be worth something by now, don't you think?"

FORTY

THE GRAPEVINE

C arter was just about to take the phone off the hook to avoid any late-night expressions of support from the guys at the station when it began ringing. He stared at it for a moment before picking up. Expecting to hear from Skeeter or Goolsby, or maybe even the chief, he was pleasantly surprised when Dakota's voice came over the line.

"You all right?" she asked.

"Sure," Carter said. "I'm great. Why wouldn't I be?"

"I heard you had kind of a busy day."

"Really? Where'd you hear that?"

"I went by the station to see if you wanted to grab a late lunch. They told me what happened."

"They tell you about the shrink?"

"Yeah."

"So now you know I'm a nut. I guess you had to find out sooner or later."

"It's not like I haven't noticed all that tossing and turning you do at night."

"Some bunch of big-mouth friends I've got, huh?"

"Hey, they're worried about you, Carter. You're lucky. And it's not like anybody's ever been committed for having bad dreams."

"Bad dreams. They don't know the half of it. Neither do you, Dakota."

"That's okay."

"You know, I don't have any idea what the hell I'm gonna do now."

Dakota paused. "I may be out of work myself. Horace took off in my plane for some place down south this morning, and he hasn't made it back."

"You don't sound all that worried."

"Carter, you know what you said the other day about keeping secrets being a bad way to start?"

"Yeah, I remember."

"I feel like we both have some things that need to be laid on the table. I was thinking we'd play a little game of truth or dare."

"Are you serious?"

"Yeah. I'm having a party this weekend, and that's always been my favorite party game."

"Mine, too, but I've always gone more for the 'dare' part of it."

"Then we'll both have to change our way of thinking."

FORTY-ONE

A DRIVE IN THE COUNTRY

Desmond finished reading Simon and Raoul's report, snorted disgustedly, and crushed the three pages of tissue-thin fax paper into an uneven ball. He walked to the middle of the holding cell he had been using as a private office and tossed the report into the toilet.

The Tarpole Flats operation had been just as calamitous as the one he and the Bottleneck police had attempted, and to add insanity to the carnage, Simon had penciled in "spontaneous human combustion" as the cause of Mackey's death.

Leaning forward, Desmond depressed the toilet's handle and sent the baffling document swirling into the town's bowels.

Skeeter entered the cell. "Whoops. Sorry about that."

"What?"

"Thought I caught you taking a leak."

"No. What's up?"

"I got the results here on those prints from the bottle you found at Kindel's."

"And?"

"They match that extra set from the bank safe. Case closed, huh?"

"Yeah, case closed."

"Guess you'll be leaving town now."

"Soon. I need to take care of one more thing. You got Carter's address?"

∼

Desmond spied Carter as he pulled his truck out of the driveway and accelerated toward the highway. Desmond hung back a hundred yards or so, following.

He slowed as he and his quarry hit the highway, letting a moving van pull between them for cover. The van, however, soon proved too slow a shield as Carter began picking up speed, hurtling toward the edge of town.

After a few minutes, Carter began slowing. His right turn signal flashed just before he whipped off the highway and onto a narrow, tree-lined dirt road, leaving a trail of dust as he sped away from the pavement.

Desmond drove a short distance past the mouth of the road and pulled to the side of the highway. He got out and looked through his binoculars, spotting the dust cloud and the truck at its head. He watched as Carter reached the end of the road and skidded to a halt next to a tow truck, which was parked in front of an old building.

Tossing his binoculars onto the front seat, Desmond locked the car and jogged toward the road.

FORTY-TWO

TOKE'S PLAN FALLS THROUGH

Carter stepped into the trading post. As his eyes adjusted to the dim light, he saw Toke leaning against the decaying bar and sucking whiskey from a small flask.

"It's a little early in the morning for that, isn't it?" Carter asked.

"It's a little early for me to be up at all. Where the hell is it?"

Carter walked to the center of the trading post and kicked the paint can aside. He patted the dirt with his boot. "Right here."

"Buried?" Toke hissed. "You mean we gotta dig it up?"

"You've got to dig it up. I'm gonna smoke a cigarette."

Carter lit up as Toke tossed his liquid breakfast aside, dropped to his knees, and began digging with his hands. It didn't take him long to unearth the swollen satchel. Pulling it from the dirt, he stood up and slung it onto the bar.

"This is it, huh?"

"Open it up. Take a look."

Toke ripped the bag open, plunged a dirty hand inside, and withdrew Carter's mask. He threw it to the floor and tried again, this time pulling out a fistful of cash.

Carter dropped his cigarette to the trading post floor and ground it into the dirt with his heel. "How much of it do you want?"

"Huh?" Toke was staring into the bag, practically drooling.

"How much is it going to take for you to keep your mouth shut about this?"

"Oh yeah," Toke said, putting the money back into the bag. He turned to face Carter, taking a snub-nosed revolver from his waistband.

"What's that for?" Carter asked.

"Well, I've been studying over it, and I don't see why I shouldn't keep it all."

"You think that's fair? I've gone to a hell of a lot of trouble for it."

"Too bad."

"You're not going to kill me, Toke."

"I don't have to, dumbass," Toke said, beginning to chuckle. "I just have to keep you off me. I mean, it's not like you're gonna call the cops or anything."

Toke guffawed so hard he doubled over. Carter rushed forward, grabbing Toke's wrist in one hand and his throat in the other.

"Hey!" Toke gurgled. "Back off!"

As they grappled, Toke's gun went off. The slug lodged in one of the brittle timbers supporting the trading post's sod roof. The timber cracked along its length and buckled slightly, filling the air with hundred-year-old dust.

Desmond burst into the trading post, his pistol drawn. He tried to draw a bead on Toke, but he and Carter were intertwined like a pair of lovestruck rattlers.

As he struggled with Toke, Carter spied Desmond standing just inside the swinging doors. His distraction gave Toke
a momentary leverage advantage, which he used to hurl
Carter into the agent. The two of them went crashing to the
floor, Desmond's gun flying from his grasp.

"What the hell are you doing here?" Carter snarled as they
got up.

"You told me not to leave town without saying goodbye."
Desmond was scanning the floor for his lost gun. He spied it
just as Toke scrambled over to pick it up.

"I don't know who the hell you are, mister, but you just
stuck your finger in the wrong pie," Toke said. He backed
toward the bar, keeping both weapons pointed toward Carter
and Desmond.

As he reached around to grab the money from the bar,
there was a sharp crack. Carter looked up and saw the timber Toke's wild shot had split beginning to give way. He
turned and hurled himself into Desmond, propelling them
both out the trading post's entrance just as the straining support gave way and brought the roof caving in on Toke.

As they lay on the ground just outside, gasping for air,
Desmond rolled over to face his savior, massaging his aching
ribs.

"Who the fuck was that guy?"

"Toke Wheeler," Carter said, sitting up. "Think he's alive
in there?"

Desmond shook his head. "I think he's goo. But how'd you
know?"

"Know what?"

"That this Wheeler guy robbed the bank. How'd you figure it out?"

"What are you talking about?"

"Come on, work with me here. I want to get the hell out of this town."

Carter stood up, brushing the dust and debris from his clothes. He extended a hand to Desmond and pulled him to his feet.

"Just playing a hunch, I guess."

"Good work. We got the perpetrator and recovered the bank's money."

"All the money might not be in there."

"Well, that's to be expected. With a guy like this, there's no telling where he blew it. Maybe at Kindel's place. That would explain that big wad of cash Goolsby found out there. What do you think?"

"Yeah, that sounds good."

"The important thing is, this is all over now. Right?"

"Abso-fucking-lutely."

FORTY-THREE

THE NAME OF THE GAME

Dakota stood behind her son, her hands on his shoulders. The boy was seated at her kitchen table, on which a huge birthday cake baked in the shape of an assault rifle rested before him. There were ten candles on the cake.

"Ready?" Dakota asked.

Brian nodded. The two of them inhaled deeply, then blew hard.

As the candles flickered, Carter, who was seated at the opposite end of the table, snapped a shot with the camera he held poised. Looking up, he saw that the candles were still burning.

"Guess we need a little help," Dakota said.

"Who's gonna take the picture?" Carter asked.

"You can manage. I don't think it'll be the first time you've done two things at once."

Carter grinned as he got up and moved closer to the cake. Dakota cued him to get ready. The three of them blew in unison, Carter snapping the picture as he exhaled. This time, the candles went out.

Dakota cut the cake. After they'd all had a piece, Brian turned to Carter and looked him up and down. "Mom says you're a cop."

"Ex-cop," Carter replied.

"You still got a gun?"

"Sure."

"Can I shoot it sometime?"

"Brian," Dakota said, "why don't you go and play that new video game I bought you. Me and Carter need to talk for a little while."

Brian got up and left the room. Dakota took her purse from the counter, placed it on the table, and withdrew the vial of cocaine she kept inside. She set it on the table between her and Carter.

"What the hell is that?" Carter asked.

"It's a long story, but I'm ready to tell it if you'll listen."

Carter nodded. "I wasn't completely honest with you when we talked on the phone."

"You weren't?"

"No. I've always been more of a 'spin the bottle' man. This truth stuff scares the hell out of me."

Dakota laughed weakly. Fat tears rolled from both of her eyes. "It scares me, too."

Carter got up, walked around the table, and put his hand on her shoulder.

"We're going to be all right, aren't we," she asked, "you and me?"

"Yeah, we are. Now that we both know the name of the game we're playing."

photo by jimmye sweat

JOHN DILMORE, JR. was born in Hattiesburg, Mississippi, in 1972. He graduated with a degree in journalism from the University of Southern Mississippi, and recently returned to the southern region of the state to work as an editor and publisher of three weekly newspapers. *Parts Unknown* is his first book.